# CAPTAIN OF THE GUARD

## GALACTIC KINGS #3

## ANNA HACKETT

Captain of the Guard

Published by Anna Hackett

Copyright 2022 by Anna Hackett

Cover by Amalia Chitulescu Digital Art

Edits by Tanya Saari

ISBN (ebook): 978-1-922414-54-0

ISBN (paperback): 978-1-922414-55-7

**At Star's End – One of Library Journal's Best E-Original Romances for 2014**

**The Phoenix Adventures – SFR Galaxy Award Winner for Most Fun New Series and "Why Isn't This a Movie?" Series**

**Beneath a Trojan Moon – SFR Galaxy Award Winner and RWAus Ella Award Winner**

**Hell Squad – SFR Galaxy Award for best Post-Apocalypse for Readers who don't like Post-Apocalypse**

"Like Indiana Jones meets Star Wars. A treasure hunt with a steamy romance." – SFF Dragon, review of *Among Galactic Ruins*

"Action, danger, aliens, romance – yup, it's another great book from Anna Hackett!" – Book Gannet Reviews, review of *Hell Squad: Marcus*

**Sign up for my VIP mailing list and get your *free box set* containing three action-packed romances.**

**Visit here to get started:** www.annahackett.com

## CHAPTER ONE

The moon rose over the forest, huge and bright.

Annora Rahl breathed deeply. Her enhanced Damari senses picked up so much: the rich scent of the trees, a small animal in the undergrowth nearby, cooking smells from not too far away.

But it was the moon that sang to her. To the wolf inside her.

The people of the planet Damar were shapeshifters. She was both woman and wolf, and both parts of her had finely honed, protective instincts.

Both were clamoring at her to protect her planet.

Blowing out a long breath, she strode down the forest path. It wound through the trees, and before long, she spotted houses nestled under the broad branches, all made of wood and glass.

The forest city of Accalia coexisted with the trees, the rocks, and the landscape. The Damari tried to live in harmony with nature.

But it was all in danger.

1

From a megalomaniac king, determined to conquer not only the planet of Damar, but their entire star system.

Annora's hands curled into fists, a sub-vocal growl in her throat.

She would not let King Zavir Sarkany of the planet Sarkan destroy her people, or their allies.

She'd fight beside her emperor and do what was required to win.

And it appeared that meant she had to head off on a mission with a man who annoyed her to her bones.

Annora scowled. She did *not* want to work with Captain Thadd Naveri of the planet Zhalto. She'd prefer to have her claws pulled out one at a time.

Laughter echoed through the night, distracting her from her thoughts. It was childish, and filled with cheeky delight. Some Damari children ran toward her. A few were in wolf form, others not. The little wolves almost tripped over their big paws. They were such cute balls of fur.

It wrung a smile out of her, despite all the musings crowding her head.

The children saw her and altered course. They ran over to her, those not in wolf form babbling greetings. A small, gray wolf planted his paws on the leather of Annora's trousers.

She scooped him up. "Hello. Are you being good?"

A chorus of yeses. The little wolf nuzzled her cheek.

A wave of affection flowed over her. She was Emperor Brodin Damar Sarkany's right-hand, his First Claw. She was known for being tough and deadly.

But she wanted this one day. A child. A family. A mate.

"Off with you." She set the wolf pup down. "And stay out of trouble." She watched the children scamper away into the night-drenched forest city.

She needed to protect her planet and her people. If that meant working with the man who made her want to punch him, constantly, then so be it.

She strode down the path toward the landing pads built into the side of a green-covered hill that towered over the city. Some of the semi-circular platforms were empty, while others had brown Damari flyers on them. One had a sleek, black ship perched on it like a bird of prey.

As she watched, a flyer flew toward one platform, its wings flapping like the wings of a giant bird. She looked back at the ground and spotted a small group waiting for her at the base of the hill.

The three tall men sure made an impact. Her emperor and friend, Brodin, was the tallest of the three brothers, but not by much. He was a warrior, built tall and muscular like most Damari. His long hair was silver-gray and pulled back from his rugged face.

The three of them were all the sons of the power-hungry King Zavir, ruler of the planet Sarkan. The Sarkany system consisted of five planets orbiting a red giant sun: Andret, Zhalto, Damar, Taln, and Sarkan.

Andret, a small, rocky planet, had been mostly destroyed by the Radiance, a giant, solar flare that had ripped through the system millennia ago. It had destroyed Andret's atmosphere, and killed the species who'd called it home.

The most distant planet in the system was Sarkan. Zavir ruled his planet with an authoritarian iron fist. He controlled what his people saw, touched, ate, and did. No one dared disobey him, or they disappeared in the night and were never seen again.

Years ago, after decades of fighting with Zhalto, Damar and Taln, Zavir had proposed peace in the system...by marrying a woman from each of the other inhabited planets.

He had three sons, and now those men—Brodin and his brothers—ruled and protected their planets from Zavir. They were united in their hatred for their father.

Brodin would give his life for the Damari. They'd just beaten Zavir's vicious warlord, Candela. And they wouldn't stop fighting.

Her gaze moved to the dark-haired, silver-eyed warrior beside Brodin. Overlord Rhain Sarkany ruled the planet Zhalto. The Zhaltons were skilled energy wielders who were fierce in battle. Rhain had recently battled another of Zavir's warlords, Krastin. He'd won the fight, but he'd lost people.

Annora's lip curled. Zavir's Zhylaw warlords were scum who experimented on different species. They used their tech to twist, enhance, and keep creatures alive well past their natural lifespans. Annora had no respect for the Zhylaw.

The final planet in the system was Taln. Conqueror Graylan Sarkany, the ruler of Taln, nodded at something Brodin said.

Tall, leaner than his brothers, he radiated an intense strength. His gold eyes sat in a sharp, hawkish face, and his black hair was clipped short. Not a man she ever wanted to see angry.

Brodin spotted her. "Annora, are you prepped for the mission?" His voice was deep and gravelly.

She nodded. "Yes." She met Graylan's gold gaze. "Thank you for supplying the ship for the mission. I *will* stop Zavir mining the genite on Andret. Whatever it takes."

The conqueror inclined his head.

"We can't let a chip of genite off the planet," Rhain said, his voice deep and authoritative.

Genite was a mineral found on Andret, and was deadly to Talnian physiology. They'd recently discovered, after Zavir's failed attacks on both Zhalto and Damar, that Zavir was planning an assault on Taln. His people were mining genite as part of his plan.

Talnians possessed formidable powers, and were able to command and control the geological forces of their planet. She'd never seen it herself, but she'd heard they could generate earthquakes, cause the ground to move, and shoot soil and rocks into the air.

"We have full faith in you and Thadd, Annora," Rhain said.

*Ugh.* That was the one little problem in all of this. She had to work with Captain Thadd "Uptight and Controlling" Naveri.

She'd encountered him on and off over the years. Whenever Rhain and Brodin had met up, Rhain's second in command and bodyguard was there. The first time she'd met him, she'd thought Thadd Naveri was one gorgeous hunk of a man. Just how she liked them: tall, big, muscular.

Unfortunately, she'd also learned he was bossy and controlling, and had no respect for her strength or abilities. At that first meeting, a Sarkan spy had tried to attack the kings. Luckily, the man got nowhere near Brodin and Rhain. Annora had made sure of it.

But when she'd cornered the enemy agent in a cargo warehouse, just as she was about to attack, Captain "Has to be in control" Naveri had knocked her out of the way and had taken the Sarkan down himself.

Her jaw tightened at the memory. He'd treated her like a helpless female in front of her team, and stolen her kill.

She'd blasted him for it later. The man had just watched her, stone-faced, with his brilliant blue eyes, and told her that it was his duty to protect not only his people, but their allies.

She'd growled and stormed off.

Since then, their interactions had been limited, but she'd learned that he was an uptight, controlling *fracta*. Actually, that was an insult to the small animals that lived on the rocky cliffs of the Dardent Valley south of Accalia.

Just this week, Thadd and Annora had worked together here on Damar to track down Zavir's warlord, Candela. Mr. In-Charge had skills, she had to admit. He was a hell of a fighter.

But when he'd carried her out of an alien ship, she hadn't been happy about it. Sure, she'd been injured, but *no one* carried her anywhere.

"I'd better get up to the ship," Annora said to Brodin and the others.

A burst of female laughter made her turn her head.

Two women walked toward them, arm in arm. One woman was tall with brown hair, the other shorter and blonde.

Mallory West and Poppy Ellison.

The two females from Earth had recently crash landed on Zhalto, right into the middle of the fight with Zavir.

Rhain had fallen for the tough Mallory West. The woman was tall, athletic, and a fighter. She'd helped the Zhaltons defeat Krastin. Rhain and Mal were soon to be married, and she was to become Queen of Zhalto.

Meanwhile, Poppy—a scientist—had been infected with the Damari virus. She'd ended up on Damar under the care of their healers.

Annora had possessed a front row seat as the small human fired up every one of Brodin's protective instincts. The man had fallen hard.

Annora hadn't liked it at first, not because she had a thing for Brodin—who was like a best friend and brother to her—but she'd seen Poppy as weak, an outsider. But Poppy had won her over. There was no doubt that the woman adored Brodin—the man, not the emperor.

"Good luck," Mal said. "Make sure Thadd doesn't get himself killed being a hero."

"I'm not a miracle worker," Annora muttered.

Mal snorted. "It's in that man's genetic makeup to jump into a fight. He can't help himself."

Annora frowned.

A hand pressed to her arm. "Be careful, Annora."

She looked down into Poppy's concerned face.

"I will."

"Your leg's all right?" Poppy asked.

Annora had suffered bad claw marks from a crazed Zhylaw cat in the most recent fight. "All healed." There was no sign of the wounds, and the healers had done a great job, but it still ached on occasion.

"Your sister will miss you," Poppy said.

Annora felt a tightness in her chest. Her baby sister, Nayla, had been taken hostage by Candela. They'd rescued her, and she was safe, but Annora still woke in the night, thinking Nayla was gone. She was supposed to protect her baby sister, and she'd failed her.

As First Claw, it was her duty to protect all Damari.

She wouldn't fail again.

Annora nodded. "I'd better go and meet Captain Naveri."

At that, Poppy gave her a look and an amused smile. Annora ignored it. She was excruciatingly aware that Poppy had caught her and Naveri kissing.

A hot, scalding, angry kiss.

"We'll see you when you return." Brodin slid an arm around Poppy, tugging her close.

The look on his rugged face... Annora felt another spike of emotion. *That.* She wanted that. A passionate love, and a mate who openly adored her.

With a nod, she headed for the elevators. Her hands flexed. Instead, she was off on a dangerous mission, with a man who showed little emotion and was bossy, irritating...

She stepped into the elevator car, and the doors closed behind her. The elevator started climbing.

A man who'd kissed her senseless the last time she'd seen him.

She blew out a breath.

Why was it the man who drove her crazy had also given her the hottest, best kiss of her life?

---

THADD NAVERI CROSSED his arms over his chest and watched the Damari workers loading gear onto the sleek, black ship.

Their shapeshifter strength was obvious in the way they easily maneuvered the heavy boxes. It looked like they had everything under control.

He turned his head, taking in the view from the landing pad.

It was a good one.

He wasn't a man to stand around admiring the scenery, unless he was doing recon on enemy positions, but even he had to admit the forest city of Accalia was beautiful.

The moonlight washed the landscape in silver. Glowing lights glimmered through the foliage—Damari homes filled with families.

Zhalto had more varied terrain—from lightly forested hills, to the flat, fertile farmlands, to the rocky abyss of the Barrens.

He breathed deeply. There was something to be said

for the lush, green scent of dense, healthy forest, however. He also felt a pulse of energy.

Unease skittered through him.

Usually, on other planets, the energy wasn't as strong for Zhaltons. But he'd been ignoring the fact that his abilities had...altered. That since he'd come to Damar, the energy here felt just as strong to him as on his homeworld.

He pressed his lips together. It would settle down. It was just a brief anomaly.

His gaze tracked back to the ship.

It was Talnian designed and built. The Talnians had some of the best starships and tech in the system, second only to Sarkan.

His lip curled. The war-like planet hadn't developed any abilities from the Radiance; they were too far out to be affected by the intense radiation. Instead, they depended on technology for their advantage, manufacturing weapons and tools of war.

And allying with the Zhylaw.

Thadd's gut curdled.

The Zhylaw warlord Krastin had attacked Zhalto, bringing terrible creatures called hexids with him. In the fight, he'd also managed to take Thadd hostage.

He swallowed the terrible taste in his mouth and fought back nausea. What Krastin's scientists had done to him...

*No.* Thadd clamped his mind shut on those memories.

He'd survived. His physical injuries were healed. There was no reason to revisit them.

He just wished that every time he tried to sleep, the memories didn't well up, like poison.

He dragged in a breath and focused on the ship again. It would be perfect for the mission. With its slick lines and black metal, it was built for speed and stealth.

Whatever bad things Zavir planned to do with the genite, they had to stop it.

A muscle ticked in Thadd's jaw. He would do whatever it took. Not just for the Talnians, but because stopping *gorr*-cursed Zavir was now Thadd's burning ambition.

"Captain?"

A burly Damari approached. He moved with the liquid prowl that all the wolves possessed. It was also clear he was well trained. Thadd suspected the man was one of Brodin's cleavers—his elite fighters.

"Yes?" Thadd said.

"The loading of the cargo is almost complete. The Talnian pilots have said we'll be good to go soon. There are a couple more pieces of equipment to load." The man nodded his head.

A low hum reached Thadd's ears. A small loading unit, manned by a Damari and loaded with the tower of boxes, approached.

"It's the heavy stuff," the man said. "Randis-repellent generators and drills. Just in case."

The randis were dangerous, ground-boring, tentacle-like creatures that lived on Andret. Not much was known about them, except that they were attracted by sound and vibration, and attacked wildly, devouring anything they could. His team needed to avoid the creatures, if possible.

The repellent fencing was from Zhalto. They used it against the irradiated beasts that lived in the Barrens. It gave off a low hum of energy that kept the creatures at bay. They were hoping it would work on the randis.

"Very good," Thadd said.

"You're a man of few words, Captain." The gregarious Damari slapped a hand to Thadd's shoulder. "I like it."

Thadd barely controlled his flinch. Since he'd been taken by Krastin, Thadd didn't like being touched. He surreptitiously sidestepped away from the Damari.

The Zhylaw scientists, at Krastin's bidding, had touched Thadd all over, cracked open his body, doing whatever the *gorr* they wanted. They'd implanted their cursed tech into his body. It had all been removed by the Zhalton medicas, but sometimes, he still felt it. He rubbed his shoulder. He kept hoping the phobia would ease. He hadn't minded being touched before. He touched Rhain and his fellow fighters in training, hugged his mother, enjoyed the odd, sweaty night with a woman when he had time.

But since his captivity, his bed had been empty. *Gorr,* he could barely sleep in it, let alone share it with someone else.

*It'll pass, Naveri.* He flexed his hand. *You're fine.*

The elevator doors on the landing pad opened, and a tall, fit woman with a long ponytail of black hair strode out.

Everything in Thadd reacted, tensing tight.

There was one single person he didn't mind touching him.

Thadd kept his face impassive. The irony was that he knew Annora would sooner slit his throat with bloody claws than touch him.

He knew, because she'd actually said that after their one shocking, hot kiss.

Thadd blew out a breath. He had no idea why this tough, very spiky woman made him both hotter and angrier than anyone ever had.

Now, they had to work together. She spotted him, and he watched her steel herself and stride his way.

She moved with that wolfish grace, too, but there was something even more sensual about Annora's walk. Something about her movements that made Thadd think of sex.

*Gorr.* He pressed his lips together.

"Captain." Her tone made it sound like a curse. She had a smoky voice he liked.

"First Claw. The loading is almost complete."

"Good." She eyed the loader heading toward the open cargo door of the ship. Several workers were waving it in.

"Then we can be on our way." She stepped closer to him, and her scent hit his nostrils. Fresh, like a cool stream, but with a wild, sexy undertone.

"Listen, Naveri, we're both in charge here. I won't have you overriding my orders, or trying to save me like I'm some pup in danger. Got it?"

He felt his hackles rise. "I have no plans to override your orders, unless they're wrong."

She growled. "You wouldn't know teamwork if it sank its claws in your ass."

"I'm aware that you're a talented, experienced fighter and leader, Annora. You wouldn't be First Claw, otherwise."

"You say that, but your actions say differently. And I hear a *but* in there somewhere." Her dark brow rose.

"But, if you're in danger and need help, I won't stand by and let you get killed."

She growled again. "I think you underestimate my abilities. I can take care of myself."

Thadd grunted.

Her gaze narrowed. "Do you have a problem working with a woman?"

He made a scoffing sound. "A good portion of my team of fighters is women."

"So, it's just me you don't respect?"

Now Thadd growled. "That's not it—"

Annora held up a hand. "It doesn't matter. Just stay out of my way, Naveri, and we'll be just fine."

Suddenly, shouts and a scream cut across the landing pad.

They both spun, just in time to see the loader and its tower of cargo start to tip toward the group of workers.

## CHAPTER TWO

**B**y *the wolves*. Annora started to move.

But Thadd beat her to it.

For such a big, muscular man, he was quick off the mark. He burst forward, then leaped into the air.

She felt a rush of energy, the hairs on her arms rising. He'd used his ability to manipulate energy to propel himself forward.

Thadd caught a box midair, then tossed it to the side. It slammed into another, knocking them both well clear of the workers.

He landed, sheltering two Damari with his body, and thrust out a hand.

A third box paused in midair, then floated some distance away and landed on the metal floor of the landing pad with a clang.

"Help," a frantic voice yelled.

Annora sprinted forward, leaping over a tumbled box.

The loader driver was sprawled on the floor, the overturned machine pinning the man's legs.

"Hold on!" She gripped the equipment and used every bit of her Damari strength.

The loader was heavy. She gritted her teeth and shoved harder. It moved a little.

"I still can't get free," the young man gasped.

Two strong hands landed on either side of Annora's.

She turned her head, and found Thadd's rugged face close to hers. His big body pressed against her back.

"Push," he ordered.

Together, they heaved. The loader moved, and the driver slid his legs free.

"Are you all right?" Annora asked, trying to ignore Thadd's proximity.

The loader driver nodded, clutching one ankle.

"Let's right this," Thadd said.

Everything the man said sounded like an order. She huffed out a breath. She couldn't get angry at him when he'd just saved a bunch of people's lives.

Together, they shoved the machine, and it landed back on its wheels. She met his steady, brilliant-blue gaze. His eyes made her think of the beautiful waters of the Duranti Sea to the east. She'd swum there as a child.

Then she hurried to the injured driver. As she checked the young man's ankle, she was dimly aware of Thadd checking on the others.

Someone laughed. She glanced over and saw Thadd nodding, helping a Damari to his feet.

There was just something about the Zhalton that

made people trust him. He'd leaped in without hesitation.

Ugh, he confused the hell out of her.

Thadd crouched to examine a cargo box, which drew her gaze to his tight, muscular ass under his black trousers.

A flare of heat coiled in her belly.

He confused her, but not her body, or her wolf. She felt every wild Damari instinct in her flaring to life.

*No.* She rose. "You should get to the healers. Let them check your ankle."

"Yes, First Claw." The driver's voice was a little shaky, but relieved. "Thank you. And thanks to the captain."

With a nod, she waved over a cleaver to help the man.

"First Claw?" The landing platform master strode over. The older Damari was stocky, with a powerful body and graying hair. "I'll ensure the last of the equipment is loaded on the ship. Thanks for making sure no one got squished."

"I'm just glad no one was hurt, Nanand. And check that loader."

The man nodded. "We will. The stabilizers must be malfunctioning."

She nodded again and the platform master hurried off, bellowing orders to his team. She lifted her gaze and found Thadd watching her.

Annora cleared her throat. "Thank you for your help. People would've been very badly injured."

He cocked his head. "Did that hurt? To thank me."

*Insufferable man.* "It stung a little, but you deserved

17

it. Now, shall we board? The sooner we complete this mission, the sooner it's over."

"After you, *thistla*."

Annora narrowed her gaze. "What did you call me?"

"Thistla. It's a wild plant that grows on Zhalto. There's some outside my window in Citadel. It's covered in beautiful, fragrant, white blooms, and thorns. Lots of thorns. I think the name suits you." He strode up the ramp into the Talnian ship.

She swallowed a growl. *You can't claw up your Zhalton ally.* She repeated it a few times.

It was going to be a long mission.

The inside of the ship was as sleek as the outside, with dark seats and cabinetry, accented with orange-gold metal. The other two members of their team sat in the main passenger cabin in the center of the ship. There was a short hall leading to some smaller personal cabins at the back of the ship. They weren't huge, but they'd be comfortable enough for a short mission.

By the wolves, she hoped this mission was short.

She had one of her best cleavers with her. Tolf was an experienced fighter, and level-headed for a Damari. He was tall, with a muscular body, and short hair in a silver-gray color common to some Damari.

A Zhalton female sat in one of the wide chairs. The woman had short, blonde hair and held herself with fight readiness. A sheathed sword rested near her chair.

Thadd's big form looked even bigger inside the confines of the ship. He talked quietly with the two Talnian pilots, who were sitting at the front of the ship in the spacious cockpit. His voice was a low rumble.

She joined him.

"Annora, this is Vash and Hagen," Thadd said.

Vash raised a hand in greeting. She looked to be about fifteen years older than Annora. Her dark hair was threaded liberally with gray and pulled back in a braid. The young man beside her screamed pilot. Hagen was young, fresh-faced, and cocky. He smiled.

"Thanks for coming with us," Annora said. "You need to stay with the ship at all times. We don't want you to risk any exposure to the genite."

Both pilots nodded.

"Vash doesn't like being away from her baby anyway," the younger man said, patting the console.

The woman shot him a look, but she was smiling. "I'm also the ship's mechanic, so I guess it is my baby." She tapped her fingers on the console. "She has speed and firepower. Should be perfect for your mission."

"Let's hope we don't need those," Thadd said. "Stealth is our main priority."

"She has that, too," Vash added.

"Are the maps with the location of the Sarkan mining camp loaded in the system?" Thadd asked.

The woman nodded. "Yes, Captain Naveri."

"Excellent," Annora said. "Our first task is recon. We need to gauge the layout of the mining camp, security numbers, and exactly what they're doing." She belatedly remembered that she wasn't the sole person in charge and glanced at Thadd. "Right, Captain?"

Blue eyes regarded her steadily. She had no idea what he was thinking. He was so contained and good at not showing anything.

"Correct," Thadd agreed. "We don't want to alert the Sarkans to our arrival."

Vash nodded. "The ship has excellent stealth capabilities. We can land without being detected."

"We need to keep some distance from the camp," Thadd said. "And go in on foot."

"We've located a plain that would be perfect for landing," Hagen said. "We've retrofitted dampeners on the ship to avoid the randis."

Thadd turned to Annora. "We'll need to wear personal sound dampeners when we step off the ship, or we'll be randis bait."

She nodded.

"We'll be ready to go shortly," Vash said. "The cargo team is finishing up."

Annora straightened. "Let's go over our plans with the team."

Back in the main passenger area, Annora watched Tolf and the Zhalton fighter eyeing each other cautiously.

She pressed a hand to the back of one chair. "Thank you for volunteering to be a part of this mission. It is vital that we stop Zavir's plans and prevent any genite leaving Andret."

There were nods and murmurs from the two fighters.

"Tolf," she waved a hand. "You know Captain Naveri."

Thadd nodded. "And this is Carvia."

"We need to work together." Annora met everyone's gazes. "The first task is recon of the mining camp."

Thadd nodded. "Vash and Hagen will stay to protect the ship."

"The randis are deadly. Our records on them are very old." Annora touched a screen set on the wall and an image appeared.

The randis had a large, tentacle-like body, with several appendages. Its skin was black and looked slick.

"The appendages have small mouths and serrated teeth. They rip and tear until there's nothing left of their prey."

"*Gorr*," Tolf muttered.

"Size?" Carvia asked, a groove appearing on her brow.

"We have conflicting reports," Annora said. "People have reported seeing small ones and large ones. We assume the small ones are juveniles. They're still lethal."

Tolf crossed his brawny arms. "Lovely little things."

"We'll wear personal sound dampeners," Thadd said. "They must be attached to you and active at all times. If you get trapped without a dampener, don't move."

"How are the Sarkans shielding the camp?" Carvia asked.

"We don't know," Annora said. "The camp is located here." She touched the screen again, and a map appeared, showing Andret's rocky surface.

Thadd shifted closer, his body brushing hers as he pointed. She ruthlessly ignored the tingles in her body.

"The camp is at the bottom of a hilly ridge," he said. "This is the only surveillance image we have."

The image zoomed in. The vague outlines of equipment and buildings could be seen through a glow of white light.

"We suspect they're using tech like Zhalton energy

barriers to keep the randis away from the camp," Thadd continued. "We'll go in and confirm. The trek to the camp will be rocky and rough."

"There's no breathable atmosphere on Andret," Annora said. "We have suits for everyone, with state-of-the-art air recycler systems. Don't leave the ship without it. Okay, who's ready to take down some Sarkans?"

"*Gorr*, yeah," Tolf said.

Annora met Thadd's gaze and he nodded. Then he looked back at the screen, staring intently at the camp. His face hardened, and she couldn't quite read the look on it. But she knew it was scary.

---

THADD STOOD in the small cabin he'd claimed and pulled on a spacesuit. He'd done some space training years ago, but it wasn't his area of expertise. He much preferred his boots on the ground, sword in hand, energy running through him.

He tugged the high-tech, black fabric into place. It had silver edging, and a small air recycler unit resting on his back between his shoulder blades. It was more Talnian tech.

His sword was lying on the narrow bunk. It was a long, straight blade that shone a dull silver in the light. He took great care to keep his sword well-maintained. It had been especially crafted for him by one of the best weapons smiths on Zhalto. He could charge it with energy during a battle, which made it faster, sharper, more deadly.

His spacesuit had a back sheath attached to it, and he slid the sword in until the hilt rested above his shoulder.

He dragged in a deep breath, preparing for the mission in his head. Then he touched the sensor and the cabin door slid open soundlessly. He moved down the narrow hall, and saw Annora out in the main passenger area.

His cock tightened, and he hissed.

Just one look at her in her sleek spacesuit and he was as hard as craxma metal.

He needed to get his response under control.

The black fabric slicked over her body. But it wasn't the suit, it was the athletic, but clearly feminine body under it that got to him. She was toned and strong, and her legs were so long. A few times, Thadd had intimidated women with his size and strength.

But he knew that Annora Rahl wouldn't be afraid of him.

Her head turned and their gazes clashed.

Thadd moved forward, willing his cock not to embarrass him. At least his suit was tight.

"We're in visual range of Andret," she said.

His pulse accelerated. He was ready for this mission. He liked action, liked a good fight. And he had a lot of motivation to do whatever he could to screw up Zavir's plans.

He moved to the cockpit. The console was awash in lights, and the pilots were focused, murmuring quietly to each other.

And there it was. The dark, rocky hunk of Andret on the viewscreen.

It seemed impossible that this planet had once harbored any life. There were lots of craters, and the surface was rocky with hilly terrain. He wondered about the Andretians of long ago. He couldn't picture a thriving, advanced species here. Old records said they'd been a very spiritual race, but any evidence of them, or their practices, were long gone thanks to the Radiance.

"Activating full stealth mode," Hagen said.

There was a shimmer of light across the viewscreen.

"We'll be landing shortly," Vash said.

"Activating dampeners," Hagen murmured.

The ship flew closer to the planet.

"The mining camp will be visible off to our right in about a minute," Vash said.

Annora moved up beside Thadd. They both stared across the rocky landscape.

"Not very hospitable," she said.

He grunted a noncommittal reply. "There."

There was a blue-white glow of lights in the distance. Yes, the Sarkans were definitely here.

"I'll tell Carvia and Tolf to be ready." Annora headed back to the passenger area.

Thadd took another look at the camp, but couldn't see much detail from this distance. He turned and followed her.

Then he heard the sound of a gorgeous, sensual laugh.

His steps almost faltered. Annora had her hand on Tolf's arm, and they were both laughing. They were so familiar and at ease with each other.

A jagged sensation cut through Thadd's gut. His hands formed fists. Were they lovers?

*No.* Annora was loyal to a fault. She'd never have kissed Thadd, even in the heat of the moment, if she was with another man.

"Ready?" Thadd's voice was a little harsher than he'd intended.

She frowned at him.

"We're ready, Captain." Carvia was checking her sword.

He saw Annora lift a battle club, with a carved hilt, and a strong, sturdy design. She attached it to a harness on her back. Tolf had a large, ornate axe already strapped on.

The Damari didn't just depend on their claws in a fight. He knew that they trained with lots of different weapons.

The ship swooped lower, and they all braced.

A moment later, they touched down.

"Any sign of the randis?" Thadd asked the pilots.

"Nothing on scans," Hagen replied.

Thadd turned. Carvia and Tolf looked focused and ready. Thadd moved to a built-in unit on the side of the cabin and opened the compartment. He pulled out a small box.

"Okay, listen up. These are the personal dampeners. They let off a low level of energy, which will block any sound and vibration."

"And keep the randis away," Tolf said

"Yes." Thadd handed the man one of the small devices that were made of silver metal. "Clip it onto your belt and whatever you do, ensure that it is always active. If the small light on the side goes out..."

"We're randis food." Tolf clipped his on. "Got it."

Thadd handed one to Carvia, then turned to Annora. She took the device, turning it over in her slim hands, studying it.

Tolf pulled on the backpack containing the explosive charges. If they got their intel, and had the opportunity, they'd blow the mining camp as soon as they could.

"Right, let's do this." Tolf cracked his neck from side to side. "I'm ready to take down some Zhylaw or Sarkans. I'm not fussy who."

Tolf's younger brother had also been taken hostage by Candela, like Annora's sister. Thadd knew that Damari could be hot-blooded in the pursuit of justice. It was in their wolf blood.

"The primary directive of this outing is recon, Tolf," Annora said. "Once we have that, then we'll make a plan to destroy the mining camp."

Tolf nodded.

"Let's move." Thadd touched the neck of his space-suit and a small, sleek helmet slid into place from the back. A quiet hiss of air reached his ears. "It's currently night on this side of Andret, so we'll use the cover of darkness to help us."

As the others activated their helmets, he touched the controls for the side airlock door. The four of them stepped inside the airlock, and once the interior door had closed, the external one opened.

"The sooner we do our recon, the sooner we get to fighting," Thadd said.

Tolf grinned. "I like your thinking, Captain." He slapped Thadd's arm.

Thadd barely controlled his flinch; all his muscles stiffened.

Thankfully, Tolf didn't notice, and just stepped out onto the rocky ground.

But when Thadd looked up, Annora was watching him intently.

He quickly turned and stepped out of the ship.

The terrain was dark, rocky, and uneven. He lifted his head and scanned the area. The landscape was like a nightmare. Where they'd landed was a rocky plain, but jagged, unfriendly looking mountains loomed in the distance.

"It's hard to believe people once lived here," Carvia said through the comm unit in the helmets.

"Yes," Thadd agreed.

"Let's get to the camp." Annora pointed. "That way."

Their small group set off. There was no sign of the randis, so it appeared their dampeners were working. *Thank the auroras.* In fact, there was no sign of any life forms of any kind.

They moved into a jog, and soon their ship disappeared behind them. Thadd lifted his wrist and studied the small screen attached at the forearm of his suit.

The ship was marked with a green dot. And the mining camp was ahead, a bright blue cross.

*Get in, gather their intel, and then make a plan to blow the facility to nothing.* Thadd thought of Zavir, and his cursed Zhylaw warlords using the genite to torture innocent people. To strap them down and experiment on them, until their screams echoed—

"Thadd?"

Jerked out of his memories, he looked at Annora. She was keeping pace beside him, looking at him with a concerned frown.

*Gorr.* "Yes?"

"I said that we're in visual range of the camp." She pointed ahead.

He lifted a hand and they all stopped. The blue-white glow of lights was visible just ahead of them.

They moved slowly now. They had reached the top of an escarpment, and he wished that there were trees or something else to use for cover.

"Down on your stomachs," he ordered.

They all dropped and crawled toward the edge. The mining camp sat down below them in a narrow valley.

Thadd stared down and sucked in a sharp breath.

# CHAPTER THREE

So much genite.

The long, deep-blue crystals filled a large crate, about as tall as she was.

That amount of genite could decimate so many Talnians.

*Claw-cursed Zavir.* Annora gritted her teeth. The man had no morals, no boundary he wouldn't cross.

She watched the Sarkan workers moving around the mining camp. Temporary buildings dotted the perimeter of the camp. They were large, rectangular structures with small, round windows set in the walls and integrated ventilation systems. They were designed for exploration and expeditions like this. They could be dropped in, then loaded back on a ship at the end of the work.

"Here."

Thadd handed her a set of optics. She murmured her thanks, lifted the device, and zoomed in.

There were dozens of metal boxes all around, their lids closed. Were they all full of genite, too?

She shifted and spotted a large opening bored into the base of the cliff. As she watched, a small loader rumbled out, loaded with more genite stacked in its tray.

She handed the optics back to Thadd. "They have a lot of genite."

He grunted, scanning the camp again with the device.

"See the large metal poles set up at the corners of the camp?" he said. "It's part of their dampening system."

She nodded. "That's what's keeping the randis out." She could see the posts just fine without the optics. They were topped with a blue-white glow of energy.

"They must have something in the mining tunnel, too," he said. "But however they're mining, they can't dampen all the vibration."

"We need to see if all those crates contain genite," she said.

"I'm more interested in their security." He stiffened.

"What?" she asked.

A muscle ticked in his jaw. He lowered the optics. "Zhylaw."

She snatched the device and held it to her eyes. The view adjusted, and she focused on two men who had to be security guards. They wore dark blue spacesuits, rifles in hand.

She moved, and a shorter, more-slender man came into view. He was waving his hands around as he talked. She zoomed in more and through his clear helmet, took in the narrow face, the trim beard, and round eyepiece over one eye. His skin had a faint blue-gray tint, and the closer she looked, she saw the eyepiece was embedded into his skin. On that side of his face, his skin was scarred, like it had been melted. Whatever had happened, he'd clearly lost his eye as well.

Annora's belly hardened. She recognized him. "Naberius."

"Yes. One of Zavir's worst warlords." Thadd's tone was devoid of all expression. "He enjoys torturing people. It's speculated he has no emotions. There is no line he won't cross in the name of science."

She swallowed. Naberius didn't mind experimenting on himself as well. "And he's in charge of the genite project," she breathed.

Thadd made a sound.

She lowered the optics and looked at him. She saw a flash of pain and anger on that rugged face before he hid it.

Annora sucked in a breath, pieces of a puzzle falling suddenly into place. "You were Krastin's hostage," she said carefully.

"For a few hours." His voice was clipped. "So I know how bad the Zhylaw are. They hide behind their science, but they're really killers."

She swallowed. He wasn't doing a great job at hiding the emotions in his voice. He probably thought he was, but her enhanced senses picked up on it.

She touched his arm and felt him tense. She'd seen him flinch when Tolf had touched him earlier. She dropped her hand and watched Thadd's chest rise and fall.

"Thadd—"

"I'm fine. I survived."

But the Zhylaw had done damage. Something told her that Thadd hadn't worked through it all.

"I can only see two security guards," he said. "There must be more."

Sarkan workers were stacking more glowing, blue genite crystals in crates.

It looked pretty. Like a gorgeous stone you could use for jewelry, if it wouldn't slowly kill an entire species.

From what she'd read, it weakened Talnians, blocked their abilities, and slowly ate at their insides until massive internal bleeding killed them.

She shuddered.

Suddenly, shouts broke out below. Annora stiffened. Had they been spotted? Workers were scurrying to the mine entrance.

More security guards appeared and aimed their rifles at the mine. Naberius had disappeared.

"What's going on?" Tolf asked.

"Something with the mine." Thadd kept staring at the entrance.

There were six security guards now, rifles aimed at the large dark hole. Several nervous workers stood to the side, clearly anxious.

Three workers ran out of the mine. Their suits were mangled, blood running down their bodies.

One's helmet was damaged, and he grabbed his throat, choking, needing air. Other workers rushed to the injured and led them away.

Screams echoed from the mine, and then a deeper sound filled the air. A chilling moan.

The hairs on the back of Annora's neck rose.

Another worker burst free, cradling his bloody abdomen. He yelled at the guards. One stepped forward and fired into the mine.

The moan turned to an enraged screech.

*Gorr. What was in there?*

Another worker staggered out of the mine, screaming. It took Annora a second to realize the man was missing an arm.

Then suddenly, a shadow moved in the mouth of the mine. Something black snapped out and wrapped around the injured man's ankle. He was yanked off his feet, hitting the rocky ground, face first.

Then he was pulled backward. The man's screams intensified, and then he was gone. Pulled back into the mine.

A second later, his screams cut off.

The six guards advanced. They all fired, their laser weapons lighting up the darkness.

"By the wolf," Tolf muttered.

"Was that a randis?" Carvia asked.

"I think so," Thadd muttered, an unhappy look on his face.

The guards finally stopped shooting and silence fell.

The injured were whisked away. Now the danger was gone, Naberius reappeared. It looked as though he was ordering everyone back to work. He pointed at the mine.

Finally, a few reluctant workers trudged back in.

"There has to be more than six guards," Carvia said.

"We need a closer look," Annora said. "In the buildings and at those crates."

Thadd's brows drew together.

"We can't all sneak into the camp, or we'll be spotted," she said. "But if I go in alone—"

"No," Thadd barked. "It's too dangerous."

She narrowed her gaze. "I'm fully capable of sneaking in undetected, Captain. And if I'm spotted, I'm fully capable of defending myself."

Tolf cleared his throat. Carvia looked into the distance.

And an interesting muscle in Thadd's jaw ticked unhappily.

"We can continue to monitor the camp from here—"

She shook her head. "Daylight will hit in less than five hours. We'd have to hold our position all day, in hot conditions. We can only implement an attack plan under the cover of darkness. If I go in now, I can get the info we require *now*, then we can make a plan to attack tonight. It lowers the risk that any of that genite—" she stabbed a finger in the direction of the camp "—gets off this rock."

Thadd's mouth formed a flat line as he looked at the camp. "I should go."

Her anger was scorching. "Because you have a penis?"

Both Carvia and Tolf made choking noises.

"Or do you just think I'm incompetent?"

"Annora," Thadd growled.

"My Damari physiology means I can scale that cliff down to the camp far easier than you."

Thadd cursed. "Fine."

"I'm glad you saw reason," she said primly, then

pushed into a crouch. "I won't take unnecessary risks, and you can provide me with eyes from up here."

Thadd crouched too and caught her arm. "Annora—"

She lifted a brow.

"Be careful."

"I always am." She turned toward the cliff. She was usually careful, except when she gave into temptation and kissed annoying Zhaltons.

Annora studied the cliff face, picking the best path down. It was all jagged rocks, which gave her plenty of hand and foot holds to choose from.

Putting everything out of her mind, she slipped over the edge and found her first foothold, then she started downward.

———

THADD WATCHED ANNORA'S DESCENT, his jaw tight.

He had to admit, while he didn't like where she was headed, she was a joy to watch. She moved so easily, with that liquid grace. That long, athletic body...

"She'll be fine," Tolf said. "She's good at this. When we were younger, Annora could sneak up on our group of friends so well, we'd never know she was coming."

Thadd believed it.

But when Annora's foot slipped, and Carvia gasped, his gut went tight.

*Gorr.* He wished there was more energy he could use on this rock. But the faint trickle of energy was so weak, it was near useless and would be difficult to control. He wished for the strong magnetic field on Zhalto. Having no strong flow of energy felt like he was missing a limb. A dull ache of nothing.

Of course, Annora caught herself and kept climbing.

She was as cool as the forest in winter.

Thadd kept his gaze glued to her. She was also the only woman in the system that he could never do anything right with. Before he'd even finished a sentence, she was jumping all over him, fire in her eyes.

She reached the bottom of the cliff. He raised his optics and scanned ahead. He touched the side of his helmet.

"You have a clear path into the camp," he murmured. "There are no guards in sight."

"Moving in now," she replied calmly.

He watched her dart forward, moving fast. She crossed the dampening field and ducked behind a building unit.

Thadd felt the uncharacteristic urge to fidget. His gut was in fine knots. He saw her pop up behind the storage crates. She opened one a crack, but from this angle, he couldn't see what was inside.

"The crates are filled with genite." She moved down the row. "All of them."

Beside him, he heard Carvia and Tolf curse.

"Acknowledged," Thadd said.

She darted across the open space and Thadd's heart beat overtime.

She pressed her back against a building, and paused. She turned and clung to the side and started to climb. He saw that she'd formed claws and jammed them against the metal. The spacesuits were designed to allow Damari to semi-shift with their claws.

Annora peered into the window. "Worker quarters." She dropped back to the ground, moving to check the rest of the buildings.

Medical. Mess. Storage.

"Found it." She clung to the side of a larger building unit. "In the security building, I can see ten guards, but I suspect there are more."

Thadd noted two guards outside, circling the camp, and heading in Annora's direction.

"Annora, you have two guards incoming."

She dropped into a crouch and hid around the building unit. "I see them."

The guards moved away, and that's when Thadd saw Annora dart toward the mine entrance.

"Annora, do not go in there," he growled.

"I just want a quick look."

He cursed under his breath. Chest tight, he watched her pause at the entrance and glance inside.

"It's too dark to see much. Even with my vision. There is light farther down the tunnel somewhere."

A muscle ticked in his jaw. *Don't go in.* He saw movement to the right. "Annora, the guards are circling back."

"Noted."

Thankfully, she pulled back from the mine entrance.

Then Thadd saw what was with the guards and froze. "Annora. They have a hexid with them."

It was a large creature that walked upright on its two muscular back legs, but could run on all fours. Its body was hairless, covered in taut, almost-transparent skin that revealed its organs underneath. Its wide shoulders were hunched, its powerful, overlong arms ended in three sharp claws, and its jaw held fangs designed to rip and tear.

Thadd remembered the stench of them—rot, decay. It had no suit, able to survive Andret's low atmosphere just fine. He saw the hexid pause, lifting its face.

"Careful, it's picking up something," he murmured.

His vision blurred. He remembered the Zhylaw scientists leading a hexid towards him. He'd been strapped down, helpless.

With a growl, he slammed his mind shut on the memories.

The guards and hexid moved toward the mine entrance.

"They're moving away from your location—"

A screech echoed across the camp. Thadd jerked his head. He saw another hexid being led by another guard.

The two creatures eyed each other, snarling. Then suddenly, the first hexid attacked, launching at the second.

As a hexid swung its powerful arms, the guards yelled.

One hexid sent the other flying into a crate. It tipped over, genite crystals spilling on the ground. The guards pulled out weapons, fighting to get the creatures under control.

"They'll wake the randis," Tolf muttered.

"The dampeners should hold." Thadd prayed they'd hold. "Annora, now's the time to use the diversion to get out of there."

"I would never have worked that out for myself, Captain." Her tone was dry, with an edge.

He looked up to the night sky. Behind him, he heard Carvia's choked laugh.

The main thing was that he saw Annora stealthily move toward the edge of the camp. When she was clear and back at the rock wall, he finally let out a harsh breath.

Thadd waited anxiously until she climbed agilely over the cliff edge. Their gazes met for a humming second. She jerked her head. "Let's move back out of range and make a plan."

The four of them shifted back across the rocky landscape, out of view of the mining camp. There were some large boulders clustered nearby. Thadd wondered what the terrain had looked like before the planet's destruction.

Annora leaned against one of the boulders. Carvia sat on a flat rock, while Tolf crouched. Thadd put his hands on his hips. "I counted fourteen guards. But there could be some more in the mine that we haven't seen."

Annora knelt. She moved some smaller rocks to mimic the camp layout. She put a small row of rocks in a line. "These crates all contain genite."

"We need to destroy them," he said.

She nodded. "And we need to collapse the mine entrance."

"Agreed." He met her gaze. "Our charges will attract the randis."

She nodded. "They will."

Tolf stroked his chin. "We need to lay them, then get out before we detonate."

"We need to set them here, here, and here." Thadd pointed to the locations. "That will cause maximum damage."

Tolf pulled off his backpack and opened it. He pulled a case out and flicked open the lid. It was filled with high-tech explosive charges. They were round, and made of a dull-silver metal.

"We'll each take five," Thadd said. "We'll divide the locations. If the First Claw agrees with the plan."

Her eyes flashed. "I agree. Thank you for consulting me."

They each took the charges. Thadd gave them all a quick lesson in using the devices.

Tolf held one up. "I think—"

The Damari fumbled. The charge dropped, and he missed catching it by a hair.

It hit the ground, and Thadd and Annora stiffened.

The device clattered and rolled away along the rocks.

Carvia frowned. "Why are you two so worried? It can't go off, right?"

"That's not what I'm worried about," Thadd murmured.

A second later, there was a faint vibration under their feet. Thadd felt a tiny pulse of energy deep in the dirt. "Back up."

"Oh, *gorr*," Tolf bit out.

Thadd leaped back. A thin, black tentacle wriggled out of the crack in the rocks.

His pulse ratcheted up. "Back."

They all moved back. Annora's body brushed his. They crouched on top of a boulder together.

The ground vibrations increased.

"Don't move," he warned the others.

Tolf stood frozen, his gaze alert. Carvia stood on another boulder.

"If the randis makes enough noise, the Sarkans will come to investigate," Carvia said.

And their plan to blow the mining camp would be shot to pieces.

Suddenly, more tentacles burst through the rocks. They wriggled across the ground, looking black and wet.

"They're just juveniles," Annora murmured.

"Let's hope mama doesn't arrive," Tolf said.

One of the tentacles slithered close to Tolf, and his claws slashed out.

"Tolf, do *not* attack," Annora said urgently.

The wolf gave a tight nod. A tentacle moved toward Annora and Thadd.

"Thadd, look."

For a second, her use of his first name short-circuited his brain. He followed her gaze.

And saw two tentacles merge into one, flesh oozing together, forming a large one.

*What the gorr?*

It joined another, and soon it was as thick as his thigh. It reared up, like a serpent. He saw the mouth at the end of the tentacle, lined with serrated teeth.

It moved closer, and Thadd pulled Annora back against him. Her back was flush against his front, and she didn't fight him.

A smaller tentacle slithered over his boot. He fought

the urge to move. He had to stay still, even though every instinct warned him to attack.

In the center of their small group, the ground bulged.

There was something larger underneath, pushing its way up.

Annora's hand gripped his, and Thadd found some control, forcing himself to stay still.

Then the tentacle pulled back and slithered off the boulder. They watched the appendages sink back into the ground.

Everything went still.

Thadd let out a breath. "It's gone."

# CHAPTER FOUR

A nnora's pulse was still jumping. She stared at the shattered ground where the randis had disappeared.

"That is one ugly creature." Tolf recovered the dropped explosive. "Sorry about that."

"The small tentacles aren't juveniles," Annora said.

Thadd shook his head. "The creatures can join together, and get larger."

*Fabulous*. She let out a breath. "Let's try not to gain its attention, or make it angry." She turned to the others. "Now, let's get into that camp, set the charges, and stop the Sarkans."

"And be long gone before the randis show up," Carvia added.

"All right." Thadd's voice was a low rumble. "Let's go."

"The cliff is a little easier to climb farther along." Annora pointed. "That section is on a better angle."

They moved swiftly over the rocky ground. The glint

of something caught Annora's eye, and she stopped. It looked like burnished metal.

"Annora?" Thadd stopped beside her.

She picked up the object. It was a tiny, perfectly carved statue the size of her finger. It looked like a woman —slender and elegant—in robes. "Look."

He took it, and it looked impossibly tiny in his large hand. "It's Andretian. I've heard some of their artifacts and ruins can be found around the planet." He handed it back to her. "Maybe she was a goddess."

"She might bring us luck." Annora slid it into her pocket.

"Do you believe in luck?" he asked.

"I believe in making my own luck, through hard work and preparation."

His lips twitched. "Looks like we agree on something."

"I guess there's a first time for everything," she said dryly.

They kept moving. She watched Tolf move with easy, long strides. Carvia was more contained, but keeping up.

"Don't you believe in your energy witches on Zhalto?" Annora asked him.

She'd heard that the Zhalton priestesses of energy had been around since the Radiance, and were especially sensitive to the energy on their planet. They could have visions of the future.

He shrugged a broad shoulder. "Nothing is ever guaranteed. You can still get blindsided by things you never expect." There was darkness in his voice.

Annora fought the crazy need to offer him some sort

of comfort. She knew he wouldn't welcome it. And her, comfort Thadd Naveri? No.

They reached the cliff. This area wasn't as steep, and they were out of view of the mining camp.

"I'll go first." Tolf slipped over the edge.

They all started downward. Tolf gave some advice on handholds to Carvia. Those two appeared to have no problems working together.

Thadd climbed with power and deliberate precision. He used his impressive strength to help him.

They all reached the bottom safely.

"All right, let's go," Annora said.

They split off, sneaking into the camp. She needed to place her charges on the crates. She saw Thadd head to the building units. Tolf and Carvia moved to the other line of buildings and the mine entrance.

Thadd disappeared from view. For such a big man, he moved well.

*Get your mind off the Zhalton and on the mission.* Annora ducked behind the crates and pressed the first charge to the underside of the closest one.

Then she heard voices. She froze.

"Annora?" Thadd's urgent whisper in her ear. "A worker and Naberius are headed your way."

*Gorr.* She dropped flat and slid under the narrow gap beneath the crate and the ground.

She saw boots appear.

"Get the crates ready. The ship is due in six hours."

She guessed that was Naberius' scratchy voice. It held the undeniable ring of arrogance and superiority.

"The more genite I have, the better for developing

the weapons I have planned." The Zhylaw gave a husky laugh. "The Talnians won't know what hit them."

Annora's fingers bit into her gloves. He was a monster. The Zhylaw were all pure evil.

"Update the inventory and put it into the system," Naberius ordered.

"Yes, Warlord."

Annora arched her head and looked up. She watched Naberius hand a sleek comp to a Sarkan worker.

"All of our flight manifests and the timetable are on there. We need to be prepared when the transport arrives."

She sucked in a breath. That was valuable information, and they needed it.

"Yes, Warlord," the worker replied again.

With a nod, Naberius turned and stalked off.

The worker started to check the crates, tapping information onto the comp screen.

Annora waited. The wolf inside her was watching, alert. A predator eyeing prey.

She hoped Thadd and the others had their charges set.

When the worker had his back turned, she slipped out and set the rest of her charges on the other crates.

She crouched behind the bulky crate on the end. "Naveri?"

"I hear you."

"The worker has a comp pad containing all the quantities of genite, as well as transport flight data."

He grunted. "We need it."

"When you're ready to go, I'll take him out and retrieve the comp pad."

"You need to copy the data. If the Sarkans know we have a device, they'll try to disable it."

"Acknowledged. Tolf? Carvia? Status?"

"I'm almost done," Carvia replied.

"I need another minute," Tolf said. "I've got two guards and one of these ugly creatures heading my way."

Annora peered around the crate. *Gorr.* The hexid had stopped, looking around like it sensed something. Or someone.

"Cursed beast," the guard muttered, yanking on the hexid's chain.

"The randis scent drives them crazy," another guard said.

The hexid loped toward Tolf's hiding spot.

Annora ground her teeth together. She had to do something. She reached up and saw a blue glow. She grabbed a genite crystal. It really was pretty.

She tossed it.

As soon as it hit the ground with a thud, the hexid's head whipped around. Its eyes glowed. It ran, and leaped up on a crate.

She ducked down, her heart hammering.

"*Annora.*" Thadd's voice in her ear. "Do not move."

She heard the hexid. It made a growling noise.

"Genite fell off a crate," the guard muttered.

"Can you get that thing away from me?" It was the worker. "I hate those foul creatures."

"You just keep doing your job," the guard said.

Annora looked up.

The hexid was staring across the camp. She followed its gaze. She could just make out Thadd's shadow by a building unit. Could the hexid sense him?

After a humming moment, the hexid leaped off the crate and headed for the guards, its long chain clanking behind it.

She let out a breath.

"*Gorr*-cursed hexids," the worker muttered. "Even with the helmet on I can still smell its stench."

The man got back to work. He pressed a button on the side of a crate, and she watched as the top locked down with a hiss.

He was getting the crates ready for transport.

*No.* No genite was leaving Andret. Not if she could help it.

"Tolf?" she whispered. "It's clear."

"On the move."

She saw her fellow cleaver dart into the mine entrance.

She wished she had her sense of smell. She hated not being able to rely on it.

It must be how Thadd and Carvia felt without any planetary energy. Like a part of them was missing.

She focused back on the Sarkan worker. She needed to wait for the right moment. She looked to the mine entrance. *Where was Tolf?*

*There.* She saw the cleaver slip out. Then he went still.

She turned her head... And spotted another unchained hexid, crouched on top of a building unit.

Its burning gaze was fixated on Tolf.

*Oh, no.* "Thadd, we have a problem."

Without a sound, the hexid leaped into the air. It hit the ground and bounded toward Tolf.

The cleaver pulled his axe off his back.

*Gorr.* Their plan was about to go to hell.

Annora sprinted toward Tolf, pulling out her club.

The hexid swung its overlong, powerful arm at the cleaver. With a growl, Tolf swung his axe to meet it.

The blade bit into the creature's shoulder. It roared, and black blood slid down its chest.

Annora ran, swung her club, and rammed into the hexid's back.

The creature went down. Both she and Tolf attacked it, swinging their weapons in unison.

As they'd done so many times before.

The hexid stopped moving.

There was no time to celebrate. Shouts broke out across the camp.

Annora looked over her shoulder. Guards were streaming out of the security building.

There was no sign of the Sarkan worker near the crates. She ground her teeth together. She needed that comp pad.

*Gorr.*

Laser fire lit up the air.

"Get to cover!" Thadd yelled across the comm link.

Annora ducked, and grabbed Tolf's arm. They ran.

More laser fire followed them.

Suddenly, an empty crate lifted off the ground in front of them. It cut through the air, racing toward the firing guards.

The guards dropped their weapons and dived for cover.

Annora saw Thadd standing at the edge of the camp, his palms raised, as he focused on the crate.

---

IT HURT.

Thadd gritted his teeth. There wasn't enough energy here on Andret to call on. It made controlling what little there was very painful.

He dropped the crate and watched guards dive out of the way.

An alarm rang through the camp, deep and resonant.

He saw Tolf and Annora running. More guards spilled from a building unit.

Annora picked up speed and attacked. Thadd took a second to watch her. The woman could fight. A powerful kick hit one guard in the head, knocking him back. She lunged and rammed her claws into another man's midsection.

She jumped up, spun, and slammed a third guard into the wall of the building. She grabbed his rifle, and snapped it in half with her hands.

Thadd's cock responded.

*Gorr.* Now was *not* the time or place.

A guard rushed him, stunner in hand. Thadd's attention sharpened. He ducked the weapon, and rammed his fist into the man's gut. He followed that with the flat of his palm into the guard's face.

The man made a horrible sound, and dropped the stunner.

Thadd reached over his shoulder and pulled his sword.

The guard's eyes widened, and he scrambled backward, then turned and ran.

Thadd swiveled. Annora was taking on a guard and a worker. There was a low growl behind him.

Thadd's chest locked. He turned.

The hexid stood, staring at him. He could almost smell its rancid scent. His hands flexed on the hilt of his sword.

The creature jumped, and Thadd's mind plunged him into his nightmare.

Strapped down, fighting against the bindings, a hexid digging into his cracked-open torso. Zhylaw scientists watching on impassively.

*Pain. Helplessness. Agony.*

The hexid slammed into him. His sword flew from his grip. He thrust his hands up, keeping the creature's jaws from clamping onto his face. He strained against it.

All of a sudden, a club slammed into the hexid's face.

Black blood sprayed, and the creature's weight was knocked off him.

Annora stood over him.

Thadd pushed to his feet. He realized his skin was cold, and rage was making his hands shake. Her gaze traced his face.

She pressed her fingers to his helmet.

Several more guards raced around a building, armed with stunners.

She pulled back. "We need to get out of here and detonate the explosives," she said. "You with me?"

He nodded. Staring into her eyes, a sense of calm hit him.

They both turned and charged.

Thadd scooped up his sword and swung it. It lit with a faint, gold glow. He couldn't charge it fully; this was all he could manage. He cut through a guard's stunner weapon.

Annora leaped, lifting her club over her head. It crashed down on a guard and the man crumpled.

Thadd and Annora spun, back-to-back.

"I think I can take more down than you, Captain."

Thadd snorted. "We'll see, First Claw."

Together, they tore into the guards. One big man who charged at Thadd was good, wielding his stunner with skill.

Thadd rammed his sword forward. The man dodged to the right, and into Annora's club.

One guard left. The man turned pale. He looked at his downed colleagues and backed up.

Annora advanced.

Then a pained shout echoed across the camp.

Thadd spun and saw Carvia, her sword a blur as she fought several workers trying to get to Tolf.

The Damari was caught in a glowing, blue net. Two guards were holding it, trying to subdue the man.

Tolf groaned. They were hurting him.

Thadd ran. He leaped onto a crate and then into the air. He raised his sword. When he landed, he cut down one guard.

The other man backed up, still clutching the net. Thadd pulled his sword free, and it dripped blood. He walked toward the guard.

The man dropped his hold on the net. It blinked off, and Tolf collapsed. The guard pulled out a small laser weapon and fired at Thadd.

Thadd used what little energy he could connect with. His sword moved from side to side, a gold blur, and deflected the bolts.

One laser bolt ricocheted and hit the guard. He fell, clasping his shoulder as he slammed back into a crate.

Thadd rammed a kick into the man's head. Once he'd collapsed, Thadd raced to Tolf.

The Damari hadn't moved.

"Tolf?" Thadd crouched.

The other man's eyes opened. There were stripes burned into his skin. "Net... Burned. Trillis."

Thadd knew the metal was toxic to Damari. He sliced the rope, yanking it off the man.

"Come on." He hauled Tolf up. The man could barely hold his own weight.

Across the camp, Annora was still fighting. *Auroras above.* He could watch the way she moved all day.

"Thadd!" Carvia appeared.

"Take him." He shifted Tolf toward his fighter. "Get out of the camp."

She slid her arms around Tolf. Thadd saw her jaw lock. The Damari was heavy.

"Go. I'll get Annora. Once we're clear, we'll blow the explosives."

Carvia looked like she wanted to argue.

"Go," Thadd ordered. "Head to the ship." He wasn't sure Tolf could make the trek back.

"See you soon." Carvia's gaze was intense.

Thadd nodded.

She gripped his arm. "I mean it, Thadd. Lately, you've been..."

He reached up and squeezed her forearm. "I don't have a death wish. I promise."

The woman nodded. She hobbled off with Tolf.

The ground under Thadd's feet vibrated.

*Boom.*

*Boom.*

*Boom.*

His muscles locked. Was it the randis?

He saw Annora and the man she was fighting both freeze. Thadd frowned. The dampeners were all still in place.

*Boom.*

A robot stomped around the corner of a building unit.

No, it wasn't a robot, it was an exo suit.

With Naberius inside.

The Zhylaw's face was visible in the center of the metal suit, behind a clear plastic shell. The suit's arms and legs were sturdy. It was built for use in mines and construction for lifting.

Naberius lifted a crate of genite like it weighed nothing. *Gorr*, the man was smiling.

He threw it at Annora.

"Annora!" Thadd yelled.

She ran, then dropped flat. The crate flew over her head, genite crystals raining down.

Thadd sprinted toward her. He pulled an explosive charge from his pocket, then primed it with energy.

Pain ripped through him. There just wasn't enough energy on Andret, and it was getting harder and harder for him to use it.

The round explosive lit up orange.

"*Annora.*" He tossed it toward her.

There was no hesitation. It was like she could read his mind.

She raised her hand, snatched the explosive, pressed the button on top, then tossed it at Naberius.

It exploded, and a shockwave flew across the camp, followed by flames.

Naberius' exo suit staggered backward.

The *gorr* wasn't dead, but he looked dazed.

He tripped on a crate, staggered, and the suit teetered. Then it slammed into one of the dampener posts.

Thadd's chest turned to rock.

*No.*

The light on the post winked out. He watched the other dampener posts flicker and die.

Naberius' suit crashed to the ground.

And a low moan echoed up from the mine entrance.

## CHAPTER FIVE

Annora pushed to her feet.

The dampeners were down. *By the wolves...*

The deep moan from the mine sent a shiver through her.

"Annora." Thadd reached her. "We need to go. *Now.*"

Naberius' exo suit was still lying on the ground.

"Wait." She strode over, lifting her club.

But the suit was empty.

"*Gorr!*"

She heard Thadd curse as well. The central part of the unit was open. The Zhylaw warlord was gone.

Annora scanned the camp, wishing she could smell. She'd be able to track the Zhylaw.

The ground started shaking. The moan from the mine turned to a deep roar. Workers spilled out, running for their lives.

"Come on!" Thadd grabbed her arm.

They set off across the camp. This had all turned into a hell of a mess.

The ground heaved under their feet. Annora tipped sideways and slammed into Thadd. He caught her against his hard body.

Tentacles burst up out of the rocky ground.

Thadd and Annora dodged. Nearby, one oily, black tentacle curled around a Sarkan worker.

The man screamed. The mouth of the tentacle reared up, then slammed into the man's helmet, smashing through it. The randis attached to the man's face.

Horror hit Annora.

"Let's go," Thadd said. "We can still trigger the explosives and achieve our objective."

"We didn't get the data."

"It's too late now."

Gunfire erupted as the guards fought back. There were shouts and screams, more tentacles bursting out of the ground.

Suddenly, the ground in front of Annora and Thadd dropped, caving in. He grabbed her, stopping her from falling into the hole. They teetered on the edge.

A giant randis tentacle exploded up out of the depression.

Thadd and Annora staggered back. Another randis burst out of the mine entrance. Its huge, teeth-lined mouth gaped. Its body arched up, then slammed down on a running worker.

"Auroras above." Thadd sounded horrified.

She shoved him. "Go."

They dodged, leaping over tentacles. The ground shook. It was mayhem.

"We need to get to the cliff," he yelled.

Something wrapped around her ankle. She tried to kick free, but it yanked and she fell on her front, slamming into the rocky ground.

She looked back and saw a randis tentacle wrapped around her leg. It was only a small one, but it was strong. Its mouth jammed into her calf.

"*Ahh.*" She felt the sting of teeth ripping at her suit and skin. She kicked at it.

It tightened its hold, squeezing her calf hard. Pain shot up her leg.

A sword slashed down, slicing the tentacle in half. The severed tentacle wriggled madly, withdrawing.

Thadd hauled her up. "You all right?"

She nodded.

"Can you walk?"

She put weight on the leg. It hurt, but was bearable. Luckily, she healed quickly. "I'm fine."

They set off again, dodging panicking Sarkan workers. She saw movement and spotted a man running on top of one of the building units.

Annora sucked in a breath. "Thadd! That's the worker with the comp pad."

His brows drew together.

"We need to get up there," she said.

He looked back. He saw the tentacles everywhere, snagging workers and tearing up the ground. As he watched, one building unit sagged into a sinking hole.

"It's got to be fast," he said.

She nodded.

He touched his helmet. "Vash? Hagen? This is Naveri."

"We hear you, Captain," Vash answered.

"Get over here. We need an evac. Randis are attacking the camp."

"We're on our way."

Thadd turned back to Annora. "I can throw you up there."

She eyed the distance. "That far?"

"I can give you a boost with my energy."

She frowned. "Aren't you tapped out?"

His jaw tightened. "I can get you up there. It's now or never, Rahl."

She straightened. "Do it."

He knelt and cupped his hands.

Annora backed up, then ran. Her boot hit Thadd's hands, and he tossed her into the air. She sailed up, and then she felt a powerful boost of energy propel her higher. Like a strong wind, except power tickled across her skin.

She saw the Sarkan worker leap from one building unit to another. She dropped, landing right beside him in a crouch.

The man spun, startled. His eyes widened. "Damari."

"Yes." She snatched the comp pad off his belt. "And you're scum."

"Hey—" He tried to grab the comp pad back. Annora kicked him and he flew off the building with a scream.

She pressed the comp screen to her forearm, tapping madly. She set her suit's system to copy the data.

"Come on," she muttered.

A bar appeared, showing the progress. Down below, Thadd's sword swung as he fought Sarkans and randis tentacles in turn. She frowned. He was moving slower than normal.

"Annora?" His deep voice in her ear.

"The data's copying. It's over halfway. I just need a bit more time."

"We don't have more time."

A huge randis burst out of the ground, rocks exploding and flying everywhere. Annora ducked.

*Gorr.* She stared at the screen, willing it to transfer faster.

"Annora!" Thadd bellowed.

"Almost there." Down below, she saw him hacking into a forest of tentacles. They were spearing up through the rocks, faster and faster. Many were wriggling toward the giant randis, which was absorbing them and growing larger.

"We've got to go *now*," Thadd roared.

The screen on her forearm flashed.

*Complete.*

*Yes.* She tossed the Sarkan comp pad and jumped off the building.

She ran toward Thadd. "It's done. Let's go."

He sprinted to her, all speed and power. But he wasn't as steady as usual. She watched him stagger.

"What's wrong?" she asked.

"Nothing." But his usually tan skin was pale, his jaw so tight it looked like it would crack.

"Naveri." She stopped, yanked her club off her back and hit an encroaching randis tentacle.

"I overextended myself. If I use energy again, I'll probably black out."

Men just never knew when to stop. She'd seen it in Brodin, as well. Her emperor would keep fighting to protect his people until he collapsed.

A large randis reared up out of the ground in front of them. They both attacked it—his sword cutting high as her club hit low. The randis jerked, black blood spraying over them.

The ground heaved under their feet and then collapsed.

Annora looked back. The large randis' thrashing was causing the ground to cave in. She slipped toward the growing depression.

Thadd grabbed her hand.

There was a whoosh of sound overhead and they both looked up. They saw the Talnian ship, like a sleek black predator, in the sky.

"Don't get too low," Thadd warned the pilots. "The large randis is agile and strong. We'll get to the outer edge of the camp."

"Yes, Captain," Hagen replied.

Thadd and Annora dodged the randis, several downed Sarkans and overturned crates.

Annora saw the ship lower, kicking up dust.

A ramp at the back lowered, and Carvia and Tolf stood on it, waving them aboard.

Suddenly, a Sarkan guard flew out of nowhere. He held a tactical sword in his hand—sturdy and sharp.

As he swung, Thadd moved, pulling his sword out so fast she barely saw it.

The Zhalton blade crashed against the Sarkan's.

"Keep going," Thadd ordered.

She wasn't leaving the stubborn warrior behind.

She waved the ship lower. She'd taken one step back toward Thadd when the ground beneath her gave way.

*Gorr.*

Her body dropped. She tried to grab something, anything, but there was nothing to grab.

Below her in the bottom of the hole was a writhing randis, its giant mouth open. Her stomach dropped.

Then suddenly, her body just stopped in midair. She hung there, held by a bubble of energy.

She looked up...into Thadd's brilliant blue eyes.

He stood at the edge of the hole, his rugged face contorted in pain.

He raised his hand.

Annora floated upward.

She didn't stop at the ground. Thadd let out a pained roar, thrusting his arms up above his head.

She flew up to the ramp of the ship. Carvia grabbed her hand and yanked her in.

Down below, Thadd saw that she was aboard, then collapsed.

"He's burned out." Carvia's face was twisted with worry. "It's too hard to use energy here. He should never have been able to do it."

"Go." Thadd's hoarse word in their earpieces. "Go. Once you're clear... I'll detonate... Explosives."

And sacrifice himself.

Annora shook her head. *No.*

---

## THADD HAD NOTHING LEFT.

The rock under his exhausted body was hard. He couldn't move. He'd burned out. His veins were stinging and his strength was gone.

At least Annora was safe. He closed his eyes. And once he detonated the explosives, the genite would be buried.

He released a breath. Annora's face filled his head. Those strong, striking features. Her fierce scowl. The tough look in her dark eyes.

He would've liked to have seen that face soft with pleasure. Hear her laugh for him.

Something landed beside him. He lifted his head.

And saw that face, set in hard, determined lines.

His brows drew together. "Get back on the ship." He wanted her safe.

"Not without you, you stubborn, self-sacrificing asshole."

"Have you been learning Earth words?" He'd heard Mallory use that word for him plenty of times.

Annora slid an arm around him and heaved him up. She was so strong.

He took as much of his own weight as he could. He wouldn't let her carry him, no matter how burned-out he was.

He saw a line attached to her belt.

"You don't get to die all heroic-like today," she said.

She sounded testy. She clipped a line between the two of them. Then she touched the side of her helmet. "Haul us up."

The line retracted.

They zoomed upward. Even with his blurry vision, and dragging fatigue, he saw the destruction below.

The randis was doing a decent job of destroying the Sarkan camp for them.

He and Annora hit the ramp.

"Go. Go!" Annora barked.

The ship wheeled away.

"Blow the explosives," Thadd croaked.

Annora nodded. A second later, muffled explosions came from below.

As the ship turned, the wind rushing past them, he saw the brilliant explosions across the mining camp.

"By claws and fangs," Tolf muttered.

The giant randis was writhing. The mine entrance collapsed, causing a cascade. The ground started caving in everywhere, the hole getting wider, everything pouring into it.

Breathing through his pain, Thadd watched building units, equipment, Sarkan workers, and crates of genite disappear.

As the ship flew away, he lost sight of the mine.

But there was nothing left. He managed a smile.

"Everyone inside," Annora ordered.

She helped Thadd to his feet. He groaned.

"It serves you right." They hobbled up the ramp. "Playing hero. You were just going to sacrifice yourself?"

"Yes. If it meant the mission was a success, and..."

"And?" She bit out.

"You got away safely."

She stared at him, her gaze unreadable.

"Carvia, close up the ramp," Annora said.

"On it." The woman walked past them.

Tolf collapsed into one of the chairs with a groan.

Annora's gaze dropped to Thadd's chest, narrowed. "You're bleeding."

He cleared his throat. "It's nothing."

She rolled her eyes and helped him into a seat.

He was more than happy to get off his feet.

"You're in pain," she said. "Using energy to save me hurt you."

He shrugged a shoulder. *Gorr*, even that small movement hurt. "It's not permanent."

She thrust her hands onto her hips. "You just had to save the day, didn't you? It was reckless."

She appeared to be on a roll.

As Annora kept ranting, Thadd caught Tolf's gaze. The man shot him a sympathetic look.

"Did I ask you to sacrifice yourself for me? No."

He cleared his throat. "I think—"

She didn't stop to listen. "We work *together*, Naveri. *Teamwork*."

"Are you done?"

Her dark gaze narrowed.

He held up a hand. "Annora, I'm too tired for any more berating."

She huffed out a breath. "Don't sacrifice yourself again, got it?"

He decided it was best just to agree. "Got it."

"First Claw?" It was Vash calling from the cockpit. "Permission to leave the planet."

"Please."

The ship shot upward. Thadd was pushed into his seat, and he felt every one of his aches and pains.

They leveled out.

"We're en route to Damar," Hagen called back.

Carvia was checking Tolf's wounds. Thadd didn't want another lecture, and pushed himself gingerly to his feet. "I'll be in my cabin."

He managed to stride out of the central area unaided. But in the corridor, out of sight, he pressed a hand to the wall. *Gorr*, he hated being this weak.

He shuffled down the hall and into his cabin.

He dropped onto the bed. He managed to unfasten his suit and pushed the top down to his waist. He was sweating hard by the time he finished.

He looked at the cut on his upper chest. The Sarkan guard's sword had caught him.

He hauled himself up, and got a cloth and med kit from the washroom. When he got back to the bed, he could barely manage to swipe at the blood.

The door opened.

Annora stepped in, paused, and her brows went up. "You said you were fine."

"I am."

She threw her hands in the air. "It's a male thing, regardless of species. They can't admit a weakness. Can't ask for help. Tolf out there has several broken ribs, and he's insisting that he's fine. You're here, bleeding to death —" She snatched the cloth from his hand.

"I am not."

She made an angry sound and pulled a stool over. She sat in front of him.

Despite the anger radiating off her, her touch was gentle.

"Thadd, this cut is deep. It needs medical attention."

"I've had worse."

Her gaze traced across his chest, glancing at a few of his scars. "So I see."

His head was feeling a little woozy. "I like it when you call me Thadd."

Her turbulent, dark gaze met his for a humming second, then she looked back at his wound.

She dabbed at it and he winced.

"You need some pain meds."

"I'm f—"

She fished around in the med kit, jabbed the pressure injector to his neck and injected him.

Thadd cursed.

Annora just smiled and went back to work cleaning his wound.

"How's your leg wound?" he asked.

"Because I'm not a tough idiot, I've cleaned it, and thanks to my high rate of healing, it's looking better."

He was glad she hadn't been hurt worse.

"What do you need to heal your energy exhaustion?" she asked.

He ground his teeth together.

"I'm on your side, Naveri."

They were back to Naveri now. "Really? You always

give me the impression you want to kill me, except when..."

Her hand stilled. "Except when what?"

He could smell her hair. Despite the mission, she still smelled like the forest. Her hands on his skin were torture.

He pressed his fingers into the bed covers. "Except when you kissed me," he finished.

"That was a mistake." She grabbed a tube from the kit and smoothed a dab of the contents over his wound. It was med gel from the planet Carthago.

"You're probably right," he said.

Her hand stilled, then she briskly pressed a clear bandage over the wound.

"You shouldn't have overextended yourself." Her voice was sharp. "And I still don't know what you were thinking, nobly sacrificing your life. Do they teach you that on Zhalto?"

That Damari temper was free again.

"I—"

"No, don't talk. You'll just say something that will annoy me."

"Annora—"

"Seriously, men just have to save the day. Do you not trust women to help? I'm really curious—"

He caught her wrist. "I picked Carvia for the mission because she's one of my best fighters. And you...you're magnificent in a fight. Strong and smart. Pure, fierce beauty."

Annora stared at him.

"But I will never stand by and let any member of my

team—male or female or other—die. Not if I can help it." His tone darkened. "And I will *never* let anyone fall into the hands of the *gorr*-cursed Zhylaw."

She shifted her hands, resting them on his shoulders.

Then, proving he could never work out this woman, she leaned forward and kissed him.

*By the auroras.*

Heat burst inside him. He opened his mouth, and her tongue slipped inside.

The flavor of her filled him, and his cock lengthened. Her hands moved across his bare skin, and he liked her touch, thought of nothing but her.

With a desperate sound, he slid a hand into her dark hair and yanked her closer.

She made a sound, and kissed him again, but a second later she pulled back.

"Don't sacrifice yourself again, Thadd. Or I'll make you regret it."

She rose and stalked out.

# CHAPTER SIX

The shower stall in the ship's cabin was a tight fit. Annora raised her face to the water, enjoying the hot spray.

She washed the mission and the fight away.

They'd succeeded. They'd saved a hell of a lot of Talnians. It filled her with a strong sense of satisfaction.

But her head was still full of Thadd Naveri.

She wondered if he'd even fit in the stall in his cabin. Those broad shoulders would touch the sides. Talnians were built much leaner.

And just like that, she was thinking of Thadd naked.

She felt a pulse of desire between her legs and closed her eyes.

Then she was back at the mining camp, sailing through the air as Thadd saved her life. Knowing he was draining the last of his reserves.

She shut off the water and dried off. Hot air blew over her body from the drying vents.

She'd seen up close and personal how selfless he was.

Her belly turned over. She was known for making quick decisions, and even quicker judgments. She wrinkled her nose. And maybe she'd rushed to form her opinions of the warrior.

She realized now that Mal was right. Thadd couldn't help himself.

He was a protector. It was in his blood and bones.

But more than that, she'd heard his voice whenever he mentioned the Zhylaw. She'd seen him frozen in the fight with a hexid.

Whatever the Zhylaw had done to him was haunting him. Possibly driving him to reckless mistakes and risks.

She blew out a breath and pulled on her clean clothes. Dark-leather pants, and a fitted, black shirt.

The man confused her, but she didn't want him dead.

And she'd kissed him... Again.

She licked her lips. No one had lit her up like the rugged Zhalton in a long time.

She tied her hair up. For now, she needed to put her feelings aside and focus on the mission. The genite and mine were destroyed, but she wanted to go over the Sarkan comp data and make sure they got everything.

Refreshed, she stepped out of the cabin, just as Thadd passed by. She found herself brushing his body.

"Feeling all right?" she asked.

He nodded. "The meds helped."

His grumpy tone told her that he didn't like admitting it. She hid her smile. "I'm going to go through the comp data. Want to help?"

He nodded.

In the main cabin, there was no sign of Tolf or

Carvia. Annora hoped they were both resting.

She found a spot at the table that slid out of the wall. A comp screen was built into the surface.

"I already uploaded the data to the ship's computer. Do you want a drink? I'm going to make some cinnamae."

He nodded.

It took a moment to brew the Damari drink, then she carried the mugs to the table. When she swiped the screen, data filled it.

"We might get some insight into what Naberius and Zavir have planned," she said.

Thadd grunted and sipped his drink. "My gut says Naberius got away."

"Mine too." At the first sign of trouble, the Zhylaw warlord had run. Abandoned his people.

*Coward.*

The opposite of the man sitting in front of her right now.

Her brain was still having trouble sorting out her thoughts and feelings about Thadd.

"I won't let them torture people and decimate Taln." Thadd's voice was firm. "We need to deal with Zavir, once and for all."

"He'll never stop trying to get his sons to join him."

"He doesn't understand what drives them. And now that Rhain and Brodin have women they love..."

Annora nodded. "They'll do everything they can to protect them."

His gaze met hers. "Not because Mal or Poppy are weak or incompetent, but because they matter. And both Rhain and Brodin are men who protect."

She cocked her head. "Are you saying I've misread you and your actions?"

"I've never doubted your abilities, Annora."

She sipped her drink. "Maybe I...overreacted. When you stole my kill and knocked me out of the way that first time we met, I lost my temper." She wrinkled her nose. "I have a bit of a temper and I'm quick to judge."

His brows lifted. "A bit of a temper?"

She kicked him under the table.

"And perhaps I was a little too heavy-handed." He cleared his throat. "And trying to impress the frighteningly efficient First Claw of Damar."

A laugh broke out of her. He smiled.

Her eyes widened. "You have a dimple."

"What?" He scowled. "Men don't have dimples. Children do."

"I saw it."

He shook his head.

"I did." She grinned. "A cute, little dimple."

He let out a growl worthy of a Damari.

She touched his cheek. "Right here."

His strong fingers circled her wrist, and a streak of heat rushed down her arm.

His fingers stroked her skin and when he sucked in a breath, she knew he must feel her jumping pulse.

"You and me... It's a bad idea," she said.

"Absolutely."

Okay, she hated that he'd agreed so quickly.

"It makes no sense. We don't like each other, we fight. You're from Zhalto, I'm from Damar."

He made a sound of agreement but kept up that maddening caress. It arrowed right through her body.

"We're busy trying to stop a warlord and his king from destroying our planets and allies."

"Right," he agreed.

He kept stroking, heat in his blue eyes. They looked like jewels. A woman could get lost in them.

He leaned closer. He smelled like man—heat, strength. She leaned toward him.

Stomping footsteps echoed from the corridor. They both leaned back, and he let go of her.

Tolf appeared.

Annora tried to clear her head. "Hey, are you all right?"

"I'll live."

She rolled her eyes. Thadd caught the movement and his lips twitched. There was a sense of humor under the stoic façade.

"Carvia's already poked and prodded me." Tolf grabbed some food from the unit and stomped out.

Annora turned back to look at the data.

"Anything?" Thadd asked, clearly planning to ignore what had just happened.

"Not yet. There are lists of supplies for the mining camp, and plans for the mine tunnels." She frowned. "There are schematics for the dampening system to keep the randis out. I'll give that to our science team. There's still more to sort through."

"Naberius is too smart and cunning to outline his plans for anyone to find."

She tapped the screen. "Let's see what intel we have

on him."

Thadd leaned closer and a picture of the trim, scarred Zhylaw appeared on the screen.

Annora tapped her fingers on the table.

"He was some child prodigy. Started scientific research at an early age."

"He's had a long time to become a monster," Thadd said darkly.

She made a sound. "Look at this picture of him when he was young."

Thadd stared at the very youthful man. It was hard to tell it was even Naberius. He was thin, with pale-white skin, no scarring, two blue eyes, and long, black hair. The sneer was the same, though.

"His skin is blue now." Annora frowned. "It wasn't always."

"Naberius is a hundred and forty-one years old," Thadd told her. "A build-up of toxins in his blood, from the chemicals he uses on himself, turns his skin blue."

Her eyes widened. She stared at the picture. "He uses tech to keep himself alive." Her nose wrinkled.

"Read on."

"He went to several Zhylaw academies. Then he was posted into exploration." She grimaced. "They gave him prizes for his scientific experimentation on other species."

"The Zhylaw see everyone as beneath them. Just test subjects for their research."

His face was so grim. Annora felt a strong urge to hug the warrior.

"There is mention of something called the Laxma Incident." She swiped the screen. "He was on a research ship called the *Laxma*. They were carrying out testing on specimens the Zhylaw had acquired."

"Which means other species they'd abducted."

"Fire broke out. Everyone was evacuating, but Naberius didn't want to lose his research data. He was badly burned retrieving it and lost his eye. Only a handful of Zhylaw made it off the ship before it exploded. All their test subjects were killed."

"Which is probably a better end for the people he'd been testing on."

Annora grabbed Thadd's hand. She felt the tension in him.

"What happened?" she asked quietly.

He stayed silent, a muscle ticking in his jaw.

"Have you talked to anyone?" she asked.

"There's nothing to talk about." He tried to pull his hand back.

She held on, and they had a brief tug-of-war.

"I survived," he bit out. "I'm healed. I'm fine."

"I'm starting to think you don't know what that word means."

His blue gaze crashed into hers. In it she saw burning pain mixed with other emotions.

Her fingers clenched on his. "Thadd—"

"You want to hear that they strapped me down? Cut me open? I was helpless. I couldn't fight back. I couldn't use my energy."

Annora held onto his hand.

"They cracked my chest open, while I was awake. Do you want all the gory details?"

No. But she wanted him to let the poison out.

"They dug around inside me. They let a hexid pull on my innards. They implanted their *gorr*-cursed tech into me."

"Thadd, it wasn't your fault."

He shot to his feet, yanking his hand free. "No more questions." His face was dark.

She definitely wanted to touch him. But he spun and strode out.

Annora sank back in her chair and blew out a breath. *Well done, Annora.*

———

THADD STOMPED AWAY DOWN the corridor.

The ship suddenly felt tiny. He slammed into his cabin, pulling in some deep breaths.

"*Gorr.*" He thrust his hand in his hair.

He should've kept his mouth closed. He didn't need to spill all of that over Annora.

He needed to get back to Zhalto.

Whatever burned between him and Annora...

It didn't matter. The Sarkan mining camp was destroyed. He'd done his duty.

He started doing some stretches from his training routines. The space was too small for most of them, but the few he could do steadied him.

There was a small chime from the console built into the wall.

"Captain." It was Vash. "The First Claw needs you in the main cabin. She's found something."

Thadd pinched the bridge of his nose. "I'm on my

way."

He quickly splashed water on his face, then patted it dry. He straightened.

He was Captain of the Guard to the Overlord of Zhalto. He had vowed to protect his king and his planet. He would do his job, whatever it took.

He headed out.

In the main cabin, he found the others with Annora. She was standing with her hands on her hips. She eyed him for a second, but whatever she was thinking, she kept it hidden.

"What have you found?" he asked.

"I found information in the data." She blew out a sharp breath. "We assumed they hadn't shipped any genite yet."

Thadd's blood turned cold.

Her dark gaze met his. "I found it listed in the shipping manifest. They've already sent the first shipment off Andret."

Thadd cursed and strode across the cabin. He started pacing. The others watched him, tense and quiet.

"How much?" he asked.

"Three crates."

*Gorr*. His jaw tightened. It was enough to do a lot of damage.

"Does it say where they shipped it?"

Annora shook her head. "Part of the data is heavily encrypted. It looks like Naberius' personal logs. I'm guessing the destination is in there."

"Can you get into it?"

She shook her head. "I tried, but this isn't my area of

expertise. Our science team might have better luck."

Thadd's skills weren't in data encryption either. He looked at Tolf and Carvia. "Either of you good with encryption."

Tolf snorted. "I'm good with my claws."

Carvia shook her head.

"We need to update the kings," Annora said.

He nodded.

"We can make the call in the ready room." She rose, moving with her liquid grace.

His gaze dropped to her legs and ass. For a second, he had the unfamiliar sensation of not even remembering his name, let alone his primary directive.

She pressed a palm to the sensor and the door slid open.

The room beyond was small. When he stepped inside, it felt tiny. Annora's scent washed over him, and his body stirred.

He shut it down, as best he could. With his muscles tense, he dropped into the chair beside her.

"I can't believe they already got genite out." Her face twisted. "*Gorr.*"

"It's not your fault."

"It feels like it." She ran a hand through her hair.

He eyed her. "It wasn't your fault your sister got taken either."

Annora's gaze narrowed. "As First Claw, it's my job to protect my people. As a sister, it's my job to keep my little sister safe."

"She is safe. I saw you go without sleep, fight, and risk your life to save her."

Annora hunched her shoulders. "It's...hard not to feel responsible."

"I understand. Believe me."

Their gazes met again. A beat of shared understanding passed between them.

Clearing her throat, she tapped the screen built into the table.

"Initializing call to Damar," a toneless, soothing voice said.

A larger screen integrated into the wall flared on. They waited for the kings to join them.

"Thadd..."

He stiffened, but didn't look at her.

He felt the faint touch of her fingers on his arm.

Why did he feel that small caress all over his skin? Why did he want her touch everywhere?

Anyone else and his skin would be crawling, and the nightmares would be rearing their ugly head.

But with her...

He wanted to pull her into his arms. He wanted his mouth on hers, his hands on her smooth skin, her long body under his.

"I'm sorry for what they did to you," she said. "The Zhylaw have to be stopped."

Her words made his gut tighten.

The screen flashed, and she dropped her hand.

The three faces of the kings filled the screen: Rhain, Brodin, and Graylan.

They all looked so different, but if you looked carefully, you noted some similarities.

They were all Zavir's sons.

And all united in the goal of stopping their father.

"Congratulations on destroying the mining camp," Brodin said.

"It didn't go quite as planned," Annora said. "The dampeners were knocked off-line in the fight, and the randis showed up."

"It was...messy, but effective." Thadd drew in a breath. "But we have a problem."

He saw the men focus on him. Graylan leaned forward.

Thadd nodded at Annora.

She steepled her hands together, resting them on the table. "We managed to copy over some Sarkan comp data. A shipment of genite has already been sent off Andret."

The faces of the kings settled into grim lines. Graylan looked away, a muscle at the corner of his eye ticking.

The conqueror looked back. His eyes were burning gold. "How much?"

"A lot," she said. "Three crates."

The kings all cursed.

"Where was it sent?" Rhain asked.

"We don't know," Thadd said.

"Some of the data is encrypted. I can't get into it. But it looks like it belongs to Naberius, and we're hopeful that it contains the location of the genite."

"It's the highest priority we get that data back to Damar," Brodin said. "I'll get the science team and Poppy to take a look at it."

"We have to find that genite," Graylan said, voice hard.

Rhain nodded. "And we have to destroy it."

# CHAPTER SEVEN

Annora closed her eyes and absorbed the sound and scents of the forest.

They were back on Damar. She'd already reported in to Brodin, and they were meeting for dinner later.

The Sarkan data was now in the hands of Poppy and the science team. Brodin's mate was eager to help decode the encrypted information.

Annora had escaped for a run in the forest.

She opened her eyes and ran.

She left Accalia behind and ran deep into the trees. Night was falling, the stars winking on in the vast sky overhead. There was no spacesuit or helmet to block her senses.

No confusing Zhalton who lit her body on fire.

She stopped and shed her clothes. The cool night air washed over her skin, then she let the wolf take over.

The change flowed over her, familiar and sweet. Her muscles stretched and lengthened. Fur formed.

Her senses shifted and changed. Everything was

clearer, sharper. Her paws dug into the leaves beneath her.

She ran on all fours, all her senses painfully acute. After the confines of the starship, it felt so good.

She still felt a looming weight on her shoulders. Knowing that the shipment of genite was out there, somewhere.

And Naberius.

She hadn't failed her mission, but she felt like she hadn't completed it, either.

She spotted a flash of color in the trees. In her wolf form, she could see the heat signatures of the forest animals. A gnalia bird in the branches of an agarr tree. A mephite in the undergrowth.

But she wasn't hunting tonight.

She circled back to where she'd started and stashed her clothes. She changed back. She had just enough time to get to the lodge for dinner.

She pulled her hair up and sucked in another deep breath. She'd go for a second run after dinner. She didn't think the tension thrumming through her would let her sleep.

Rhain and Mal were back on Zhalto. Graylan had left for Taln. But Thadd and Carvia would be at the dinner.

She strode back into the city, along the main path. She passed the guest cabins tucked in under the trees.

There were flashes of light from the aconis trees. They absorbed the light of the sun during the day and glowed at night. They swept all the way up the side of the hill. So beautiful.

Then she saw gold light swirling, and her steps slowed.

She made out Thadd's tall form. He had his sword in hand, moving in some sort of training exercise.

His body was powerfully built, and he moved like a warrior. He lunged, swinging his sword in an arc. It was charged with energy, glowing gold.

She knew that he could access energy here on Damar. Not as much as on Zhalto, but she guessed this was his version of shaking off the mission, like she had by going for a run in her wolf form.

He kicked, then stabbed that deadly blade forward. His movements were fluid, strong.

Desire coiled in her belly. She felt a rush of heat between her legs.

She swallowed. Normally, she was upfront about her desires. She was a wolf and a woman. Pack was everything, and they shared affection freely. She held out hope that one day she'd find her mate, but she knew it didn't happen for all Damari. But many were in committed relationships and marriages, and no one had any hangups about sharing a consensual relationship.

Her parents were mated. They were crazy in love. Her childhood was littered with memories of laughter and affection, and catching her parents kissing in the kitchen.

They were artists. Her father was a skilled carver, and her mother designed stunning clothes. They'd been bewildered to get an intense, tough daughter who liked to fight and was driven to protect. But she never doubted their love, even if they didn't fully understand her.

Annora stared at Thadd, and watched the sword cut through the air. Another kick, another slice of the blade.

He was a man who fully understood the beauty of a good fight and had a driving need to protect his people.

He paused, and looked back over his shoulder. Their gazes locked.

She wanted to cross the space and touch him.

Maybe they should scratch this itch.

She gave a mental scoff. Calling it an itch was like calling a raging forest fire a little smolder.

"Annora?"

She dragged her gaze off Thadd. Some of the cleavers were heading up the path toward the lodge. They waved at her.

She strode in their direction. She didn't look back at Thadd, but she felt him watching her.

Inside the long, wooden lodge, a hubbub of conversation echoed around the long tables.

Most of the cleavers were at the head table. She spotted Tolf showing Carvia where to get food. The scent of roasted fowa filled the lodge. Annora's belly rumbled. She loved the succulent meat.

She was met by other cleavers, asking questions about the Andret mission. She answered their queries, then filled her plate with meat, berries, potatoes, and salads, and headed to the table.

"So they got genite off-world?" Darrah, a young, strong cleaver about seven years her junior asked. He was handsome, easy-going, and a dedicated fighter.

"Yes. Unfortunately. But we have the data and since

it's encrypted, Poppy is helping the science team to try and crack it."

"Our soon-to-be empress is a woman of many talents," a female cleaver said with pride.

"She is." Poppy was a genius, but she'd won Annora over because she was so in love with Brodin.

He was dedicated to the Damari people, but he deserved someone who just saw him, the man.

"Annora." Darrah sat beside her. He leaned in close. "Come to my bed tonight." His voice was low, deep.

The young cleaver had shown his interest a few times before. She'd considered it. He was handsome, fit, but seemed so young.

"Darrah, I have to—"

"I can sense your need. My wolf is going crazy." His green eyes glowed.

She was too much a wolf to be embarrassed. She was used to a nosy pack poking their noses into each other's business.

"Let me give you pleasure, release." He touched her hair.

It would be easy with Darrah. No pressure or expectations.

Something made her look up.

Thadd had entered the lodge. He walked slowly, all sheathed strength and power. He was glaring at Darrah with an undertone of pure male anger.

She yanked her gaze away. She'd always been honest with herself, and she wouldn't start lying now. "That desire isn't for you, Darrah. I'm sorry."

The young cleaver sighed. He was disappointed, but not heartbroken.

He leaned over and kissed her cheek, and she felt Thadd's gaze like a laser on them.

"I hope the Zhalton appreciates you."

Her belly tightened. "I have no idea what you're talking about."

Darrah grinned. He looked so cocky. "Sure."

"Go." She shooed him off.

She started to eat, nodding at the cleavers across from her. Brodin and Poppy's seats were empty.

"Any word on the data?" she asked.

Jennete, another cleaver, shook her head. "Poppy is obsessed with solving it. Brodin's looming over her, brooding, and worried she's working too hard."

That sounded like Brodin. Poppy had barely survived the fight with the warlord Candela. It had left her mate extremely overprotective.

Annora ate her dinner. She saw Tolf and Carvia had snagged Thadd. The trio sat at the end of the table.

She snuck a few glances at him. His color looked better. Carvia had said the stronger magnetic field on Damar helped recharge their abilities.

Annora shifted in her seat. Her skin felt hot. It had been so long since she'd shared the sheets with anyone. She wanted to blame that for her reaction to Thadd.

But it was the cursed Zhalton and his big, strong body that was to blame. His confidence. The way he fought.

And hell, even when he annoyed her with his heroics and bossiness, she still admired him for it.

She blew out a breath.

Right now, she had to wait for Poppy to break the encryption. Annora hated just sitting around. As soon as they had the location of the genite, she needed to be ready to go and destroy it.

And maybe, she should think about scratching this very annoying itch and getting the distracting Zhalton out of her system.

Her bite of fowa meat threatened to lodge in her throat. Those were very dangerous thoughts.

She rose. She needed some space and cool air. She called out her goodbyes. She needed another hard run, perhaps a swim in a cold river.

She stepped out of the lodge, and breathed in the night. She toed off her shoes and then jogged toward the trees, turning toward a harder, rougher section of the forest that most Damari avoided.

She needed a challenge, and she didn't want to run into anyone.

She pumped her arms and legs, and ran.

---

THADD EXITED THE LODGE, searching for the dark-haired woman he couldn't get off his mind.

There was no sign of Annora in the darkness. The lights of Accalia twinkled through the trees.

He spotted her shoes, and detected the faint trace of her energy. He studied the dense trees.

She'd gone for a run.

He didn't hesitate. He broke into a jog and followed her.

The trees swallowed him. His vision wasn't as good as the Damari, but with the dappled moonlight, he could navigate the forest just fine.

He felt the pings of energy of small animals, heard rustles in the bushes. He followed a narrow path. The terrain turned steeper and was dotted with small boulders.

*Where was she going?*

Thadd fell into a quick run. His muscles relaxed. He actually felt pretty good. Since Krastin's attack on Zhalto, the torture, then helping here on Damar with Candela, he hadn't had any downtime.

He breathed deeply, and smelled leaves, sap, flowers. He splashed through a small creek, following the rich, strong energy trail.

There was a break in the trees. The moon was high in the sky, shining down. His gaze caught on a ribbon of a wide river that split around a small island filled with trees that were glowing a rich purple. The leaves were all lit up with light.

*Beautiful.*

Something flitted around him. A small fly, glowing gold. He turned and followed Annora's trail.

He wasn't sure what he'd say to her. They would probably argue. But, he was drawn to her and he couldn't stay away.

And if she was meeting with that young wolf who'd been drooling all over her in the lodge...

Thadd growled. He'd rip the man's arms off.

Her energy was growing stronger, and that's when he heard water.

A waterfall.

A second later, he stepped out of the trees and saw her.

She'd shed her trousers and stood only in her white shirt, stretching her arms above her head.

His cock went as hard as craxma metal in an instant.

She whirled, her dark eyes widening. "You tracked me?"

He nodded.

Her eyes narrowed. "Even our best cleavers would've had trouble with that, and you don't have our sense of smell."

Thadd took another step forward. He was pulled to her like a magnet. "I tracked your energy signature. You leave a strong trail."

She sucked in a breath. They'd worked together to find Candela's lair, so Annora knew what he could do.

"Why did you track me?"

*Gorr*, he wasn't sure he had an answer for that. Compulsion. A cursed addiction that was growing under his skin.

Thadd scanned the clearing. "I half expected to see that young, eager pup here."

There was no way anyone could miss the edge to his voice.

Her eyebrows winged up, a flash of confusion on her face. Then she crossed her arms. "Darrah? He's hardly a pup."

"He touched you." Thadd's words were a growl.

She took a step closer. "You have no say over who touches me, Naveri."

He growled for real and closed the distance between them. "Yes, I do, and you know it."

She angled her chin, eyes sparking. "Most of the time I'm not even sure you like me, or if I like you."

"Your body likes me just fine."

She hissed. "We have a *mission*. One that isn't over."

*Gorr*. She was right. He thrust a hand into his hair.

Then she closed the small gap between them. The scent of her taunted him. Pure woman. Strong woman.

She challenged him at every step.

Then once again, Annora Rahl shocked and confused him.

"But I think we should clear our heads," she murmured.

"What?" he frowned.

"Get this out of our system." She pressed her palm over his bulging cock.

Thadd groaned, sensation ripping through him. She palmed him, her lips parting.

"Annora—" His voice was gritty.

"Shut up and kiss me, Naveri."

His control snapped. He circled an arm around her and dragged her flush against him.

She pressed both hands to his chest. Then he crashed his mouth down on hers.

*Auroras above*. That sharp, sexy mouth opened for him.

Thadd kissed her deeply, plunging his tongue inside that tempting mouth he wanted to possess.

She made a sexy sound in her throat and kissed him back.

They attacked each other. He hauled her closer, felt the prick of her claws.

She kissed him back with tongue and teeth. Taking from him as much as he took from her. It was a wild struggle for dominance, and Thadd had no idea who was winning the battle.

With women, he always kept a thread of control. He was a big man, a trained fighter, and he liked being in control.

But this woman seemed to blow all that away, leaving just his raging desire for her.

"I bet you're wet for me, aren't you?" he growled.

Annora sucked in a breath, her fingers tightening on his shoulders.

"And not for that pup who wanted you, but for *me*."

"Naveri—"

"You'll say my first name when you come on my cock, Annora. You'll scream it."

Those dark eyes flashed. "Cocky, arrogant, and bossy."

He slid a hand into her thick hair. "Aroused, confident, and in charge."

He took that mouth again. She bit his lip, drawing blood. They both groaned. He slipped a hand under her shirt.

There was no underwear to get in his way, thank the auroras. He reached between her sleek thighs, rubbing a knuckle through the wet heat he found. She was soaked.

She moaned, moving on his hand. He stroked her folds. "By the auroras, Annora, you want me. You're so wet for me."

"Stop talking," she choked out. "You'll ruin it."

Thadd sank a finger inside her. The sound she made was music to his ears. She rode his hand, and he thrust another finger inside, stretching her.

In the moonlight, he saw her pupils dilate, and she hitched one long leg around his hip.

So hot. So gorgeous.

She wanted him. Need shot through him, driving his blood hotter. She was unafraid to show her desire, her sexuality, so wild and sexy. There were no coy games or flirtatious teasing.

She slid her hand down his body and she squeezed his cock.

He groaned. "You like the feel of it?" His lungs and blood were burning. "Are you picturing it here?" He thrust his fingers into her.

She gave a husky cry, her hips jerking on his hand. "Make me come, Naveri."

"Say my name." He found her clit and rubbed it.

She cried out. She was close.

Thadd slowed his strokes, and her next sound was part mad, part desperate.

He let his gaze trace her strong face. "Say my name."

"Finish what you started." Her cheeks were flushed, her eyes sparking.

He'd never seen anything or anyone so beautiful.

Her hand closed around his wrist, trying to move him.

"*Naveri*," she growled.

"Not that name, Annora."

Her eyes closed, that strong leg tightening on him, and her hips jerked.

"Open your eyes and look at me," he murmured.

Her eyes snapped open, the dark depths dragging him in.

"Thadd. *Please.*"

Elation filled him. He thrust his finger into her tight warmth, his thumb at her clit.

He watched the orgasm tear through her. She cried out—his name—her body shuddering.

So, so gorgeous.

Her leg dropped. He pressed a quick kiss to her mouth and pulled his hand free.

It almost hurt not to touch her.

She stepped back, her face flushed but unreadable. Then she unbuttoned her shirt and let it drop on the grass.

Thadd hissed in a breath. High, firm breasts, a toned body. She was built for speed with underlying strength.

His cock hurt so much.

A faint smile touched her mouth. She stroked a hand down her body—breasts, belly, mound.

Then she turned and ran. She sprinted toward the edge of the waterfall and his heart clenched.

Then she leaped off the top of the waterfall in a graceful dive.

# CHAPTER EIGHT

Her body sliced into the water.

Annora rose, flicking her head back. Her body was still humming.

*Gorr*, she had just let Thadd Naveri make her orgasm.

*What had she been thinking?*

Well, truth be told, she hadn't been thinking at all, but her body had liked every firm touch.

Around the pool at the base of the waterfall, luminescent plants glowed. She looked up. There was also faint luminescence glowing in the water, too, lighting up the waterfall like a fairytale. It glowed with a soft, turquoise light. A night flower was blooming nearby, its lush scent filling the air.

Then she watched a big body dive off the top of the waterfall.

Her chest hitched.

Even in the darkness, she saw he was naked. His large, powerful body cut through the air.

Annora sucked in a breath. She hoped he timed his jump right. The pool wasn't huge, and it was rimmed by flat rocks. She'd been swimming here for years and knew it well.

But she didn't need to worry. Thadd dived cleanly into the pool.

Water lapped against her, and she couldn't look away as he rose.

Everything inside her clenched. The moonlight and luminescence highlighted every hard muscle. He looked like the warrior he was—wide shoulders, slabs of muscle on his chest, an abdomen that looked like it was carved from stone.

He was built for power and endurance. A man who could easily swing a sword and keep it up for hours. A man who would have no problem keeping up with her.

He moved toward her.

Heat pooled in her belly. She wasn't sure this was a good idea. She still wasn't sure she even liked him.

But she couldn't move. Couldn't stop.

The wolf inside her felt wild and needy. She wanted this warrior.

Water ran down his tanned skin. His wound was still raw, but healing. Her gaze skated over his other scars. For her, they just added to his appeal.

"You're so gorgeous, Annora." There was grit in his voice.

He stopped, with just the tiniest distance between them. He reached out and touched a strand of her damp hair.

She pressed her hands to his chest, her face close to the wall of muscle and breathed in his scent.

"Kiss me," he ordered.

"You are so bossy."

He gripped her chin, and she sucked in a breath.

"I think you like it," he said. "You like me taking some of the control. You always have to be in charge, taking care of things, having all the answers for everyone. Just let it go for a little while. Let me take the weight."

Annora's heart rapped against her ribs. All of that was true, and she liked her job and was good at it. But sometimes, she did wish for a break.

Thadd understood. She heard it in his voice. He essentially did the same job as her, protecting everyone, subverting his own needs and fears to be strong for everyone else.

His fingers tangled in her hair, and tugged until she felt the sweet sting on her scalp. If it was any other man, she'd knock his hand away.

But she didn't. Her blood was so hot, scalding in her veins.

"Kiss me," he ordered again.

*Gorgeous, arrogant warrior.* "Make me."

Something flared in those brilliant, blue eyes. The corner of his lips quirked.

It wasn't quite a smile, but it was close. It made her realize that while he'd never been much of a smiler, she hadn't seen him really smile in a long time.

He dragged her closer, and their bodies pressed together. The feel of his chest against her nipples was so good. It made them even harder.

One big hand cupped her breast, and rolled one nipple between his fingers.

Annora couldn't stop her moan.

He moved them backward through the pool. "Kiss me." His head lowered, his warm breath on her lips.

"Say please," she whispered.

"So stubborn." He tugged her hair. "Please."

She kissed him.

His tongue slid inside. A long groan rumbled through his chest, and he pulled her closer.

*By the wolves.* Annora lost track of everything except him. His touch, his taste, his heat. She felt cool rock bump against her ass.

He lifted her onto the flat surface, and her gaze snagged on his cock.

*Oh, yes.* He was big all over. His cock was hard, long, and very thick. Perfectly matched to the rest of him.

"Like what you see?" he rumbled.

She looked at his face, and saw the same need stamped on his features that she felt in her belly.

She was out of control. She wasn't sure she liked it. She needed to take some of the power back, or Naveri would get ideas that he could boss her around all the time.

"I like that mouth of yours." She let her legs fall apart, and saw him go alert. "I want it between my legs."

He growled. "Now who's being bossy?"

"Let's see how good you are, Naveri."

He moved, gripping her thighs. "Say my name."

"This again?"

His fingers dug into her thighs. One hand moved

upward, tantalizingly close to where she needed him to touch her.

"Say it. Then I'll have you begging me to make you come."

Annora sucked in a breath. "I don't beg."

"You will for me."

Who knew there was such a sexy beast under the stoic warrior exterior?

And why did it turn her on so much?

"Put your mouth on me... Thadd."

Shocking her, he lowered himself into the water, between her legs. His head was level with her slick core.

"Ready, my stubborn wolf?"

"Less talking, more—"

He pressed his mouth to her.

*By the...* She bit back a moan. He used his tongue, mouth, and teeth. He didn't hold back, working her like she was a feast, and he was starving.

Soon, she was writhing, her cries echoing across the pool.

She wrapped her thigh around his head, lifting up to that clever mouth. His tongue stabbed inside her.

Annora moaned. "It's... I'm..."

Had a man ever left her speechless before?

"You're going to beg me." His mouth lifted and he nipped her thigh.

She jolted. "Don't stop."

He rose, his mouth on hers, and water dripped off his body and onto her skin. She tasted herself on his lips.

"You need to say, 'make me come, Thadd.'"

She bit his lip, and clamped her hands on his muscular ass. "Do it."

His mouth traveled down her body. He lightly bit one nipple, scraped his teeth over her belly, and pressed a kiss to the damp curls covering her mound. "Beg me."

"You *gorr*-cursed—"

He pinched her clit.

*Oh...oh.* She needed to come. She needed the pleasure and release. She was trembling on the edge.

"Let me pleasure you," he murmured. "Say the words, Annora."

She glared at him. "Asshole."

"Often. So I'm told." He sank a finger inside her.

She moaned.

"Just say 'please make me come, Thadd.' That's all, and then I'll take care of the rest and give you what you need."

She stared into those brilliant blue eyes. "Please make me come, Thadd."

He smiled, pure pleasure and satisfaction on his face.

He lowered his head. His mouth sucked on her clit, his fingers thrusting inside her.

It was only seconds before she came. An intense, searing orgasm hit her.

She imploded, arching up, her body shaking underneath the lash of pleasure.

And she cried out his name as she did.

––––––––

NEED POUNDED THROUGH THADD. He could barely think or speak.

His gaze ran over Annora's lax body draped on the rock. All he could think about was being inside her.

He reached out and flipped her over onto her belly.

"Thadd—" Her voice was a little husky.

Because of him.

He pressed a palm to the center of her back, and she made a sound that arrowed inside him. Her skin was so smooth. He stroked it. He liked the contrast of tough, strong woman and soft skin.

He stroked down over her ass. He wanted to take his time to explore, but the desire pounding inside him was too strong. He shoved her legs apart and circled his throbbing cock. He bumped against her, and she moaned.

"Hurry up," she panted, pushing back, trying to take control.

He leaned over her and nipped her ear. "I'm deciding how hard, how fast, and when you come again."

She growled. "Naveri—"

He bit her earlobe.

"Thadd," she amended.

He thrust inside her.

Annora cried out his name, her body stretching to take him. He straightened and gripped her hips, holding her in place as he moved inside her.

Every slide felt so good. The tight, hot clasp of her body was better than anything he'd ever felt. Pleasure was like hot energy driving down his spine to his cock.

But Thadd realized it wasn't enough.

He needed to see her face, wanted to watch when she came.

He pulled out.

"What? *No.*" Her voice was a growl. "Naveri, don't stop."

He flipped her over, sitting her right at the edge of the rock.

"Not planning to stop, my sweet *thistla.*"

Her hands gripped his shoulders, and he felt the prick of her claws.

He liked it. Liked her passion, her wildness, her strength. She kept it controlled most of the time, but not right now with him.

He notched the head of his cock between her legs, and heard her breath hitch. His gaze collided with hers, then he pushed inside her.

*Gorr.* Watching the emotion on her face made him get even harder. She made a choked sound, then he was deep inside her.

She wrapped her long legs around him, her claws digging into his back.

"Annora, you feel so good. Hold on."

He pulled out and thrust back in. He found the right angle that had her gasping. His control bled away, and he hammered into her, not holding back.

He needed this. Needed her.

She took it, giving back, meeting him thrust for thrust.

"Thadd. I'm close."

"Good." His thrusts were rough, the water splashing around him.

She shattered. Her scream echoed over the pool. She threw her head back, her hair falling in a long sheet of black. Pleasure was stamped on her face, her body shaking, and he felt the sting of her claws on his back.

Her inner muscles clamped down on his cock, triggering his own release.

Thadd let out a low roar, but he couldn't stop, and wave after wave of pure pleasure inundated him as he poured himself inside her.

They stayed there, their heaving breaths the only sounds around them.

"Well." Annora pushed him back a step.

Thadd hoped his legs would hold him up. She hopped off the rock, standing waist deep in the water.

His gut clenched. She looked like some witch from legend, who haunted the forest streams of Zhalto, luring men to their deaths with a smile on their faces.

His gaze fell on her beautiful breasts. Firm, topped with deep-pink nipples. He hadn't had a chance to lavish them with attention. His cock jerked. And he imagined sliding his cock between them.

*Gorr.* How could he feel any desire so soon after coming so hard inside her?

"It's good we did that." Her voice was brisk, businesslike. "Got it out of our systems."

He stilled. She was trying to throw up walls again.

"It's not out of my system," he growled.

Her head jerked. "Naveri—"

"You screamed Thadd when you came on my cock and scratched up my back a few moments ago."

Color filled her cheeks. "Well, I'm done." She sloshed through the pool, heading toward the edge.

*Oh, no.* They so weren't done.

He didn't know what it was about her that made him unable to stop thinking about her. She pushed him. Challenged him.

He followed. When he stepped out of the water, he was gratified that her gaze moved down his body.

Thadd hid his smile. "Let's have a little challenge."

"Challenge?" Her gaze hit his.

He nodded. "We go for a run. If I track you down, I get to do whatever I want to you for the rest of the night."

She raised a brow. "And if you don't?"

"You can do whatever you want to me." As he said the words, he tasted the faint tang of bile. He'd vowed never to let anyone do anything to him again.

But this was Annora. She wasn't a Zhylaw warlord. If she was going to hurt him, she'd come at him head on.

He saw her watching him with a far-too-perceptive gaze.

He cleared his throat. "If that includes leaving me lost in the forest for the night, so be it."

"You seem to have a pretty good sense of direction. But I know this forest, and I'm Damari."

"And I'm a Zhalton warrior." He felt a smile tug his lips. "And I have a very enticing incentive."

She closed the gap between them. He desperately wanted to touch her.

"I accept your challenge." She spun and took off at a run.

Those legs and that ass. His cock was hard again.

She disappeared into the trees.

Excitement—hot and brutal—filled him. When was the last time something had pushed all thoughts of duty as well as his nightmares out of his head?

His need for this woman seemed capable of that.

He took a deep breath and ran into the forest.

Conscious that he was naked, he avoided contact with any bushes. A few had spikes.

He picked up Annora's energy. But she didn't make it easy. He hit a rough patch of ground, and went through some dense vines. He was breathing hard, running fast. He wanted to catch his prey.

His prize would be worth it.

His body still throbbed with the pleasure of touching her, being inside her, making her come.

He leaped over a fallen log. Running naked in the forest felt free, wild.

Not two words anyone would use to describe him.

He saw a glow of light ahead. He slowed. Annora's energy was strong, but something else was giving off energy too.

He pushed some vines aside and sucked in a breath.

It was like something out of a fantasy.

The tree branches spread overhead, dense and green. Dangling from them were flower-laden vines that glowed with a deep purple light. That was what was giving off the energy.

His clever wolf. She'd used these to mask her energy signature.

He walked into the beautiful glade. He could still sense Annora's energy, but couldn't pinpoint what direction it was coming from. He plucked a flower and smelled it.

Suddenly, a weight dropped from overhead and hit his chest.

He fell back on a bed of soft, moss-like grass.

Annora straddled him. "I caught you."

The purple light made her even more beautiful. "I was chasing you."

"But I'm the one on top." She leaned down and nipped his jaw.

He clamped a hand on her hip and groaned.

"That means I'm in charge," she said.

He felt a surge of desire. "We'll see."

She pressed a kiss to his chest. "You've got a very nice, hard body, Thadd." She scraped her teeth on his rib cage. "I like hard."

As she moved lower, tormenting him, Thadd stared up at the glowing vines and gave himself up to her and the pleasure.

# CHAPTER NINE

Annora woke to the unfamiliar sensation of a hard, warm body behind her.

She stayed still, but his scent was already in her senses. By the claws, it was in her skin.

She'd spent the entire night with Thadd Naveri's very large cock inside her. She squeezed her eyes closed.

Usually, when she took a lover, she didn't hang around to sleep with them. After a sweaty tussle, she liked her solitude and her own space.

She shifted, and a strong arm pulled her back against that body, with his hard cock nestled against her ass. She waited a beat, but realized he was still asleep.

She stayed there a moment, enjoying it. He held her easily, and it made her heart squeeze. She knew he wasn't a big fan of touching at the moment.

Except her. He liked touching her and having her touch him.

Dawn light was filtering through the trees. The radia vines would've stopped glowing hours ago. She and

Thadd were sleeping in a scout hideout. It was a wooden platform hidden in the tree canopy. She knew the location of every single one scattered throughout the forest surrounding Accalia. She was in charge of the roster for the scouts who used them, and the Damari fighters who kept them stocked.

She and Thadd were sleeping on a pile of furs. She pulled in a breath.

They'd had their night together. They'd scratched their itch.

So why did she still feel the insistent beat of desire in her belly?

Carefully, using every one of her Damari skills, she slid away from Thadd.

She instantly missed his warmth, but shoved the thought away. She moved to the wooden box of spare clothes, and found pants and a sleeveless black top her size. As she pulled them on, she noted the bruises on her skin, and the bite mark on the side of her breast. She reached up and touched a tender spot on her neck. She was covered in evidence of their night together.

When she turned back, Thadd had shifted on the furs, lying face down.

Annora sucked in a breath. She'd left her mark as well. There were deep claw scratches on his back.

She felt heat in her cheeks. She'd really been lost in the heat of their loving to do that.

But it was over now.

She needed to get back and check in with the cleavers. See if Poppy had had any luck decoding the Sarkan data.

Her gaze snagged again on that hard back, all those sculpted muscles. She forced herself to turn away. The man was smart and skilled. He'd find his way back to Accalia.

She didn't bother with the rope ladder. She leaped out of the tree and landed in a crouch.

She took off at a run.

The clean air and sunlight cleared her head. As she found her stride, she felt delicious twinges, most noticeably between her legs. She still felt him there.

*Put it aside, Annora.*

She pushed for more speed. She was panting, her skin covered in a light sheen of perspiration when she reached the city.

She headed straight for her cabin. She needed to shower before nosy wolves noticed the male scent on her.

She was almost at her door when a slim figure stepped out of the trees.

"There you are." Her sister Nayla walked over. "I tried knocking, but there was no answer."

"Um, I went out for a run." Her sister was a teenager and had a boyfriend, but Annora liked to pretend her baby sister knew nothing about men and sex.

Nayla's eyebrows went up, a smile on her lips. "So why do you smell like yummy male, and have sex hair, and are wearing borrowed clothes?"

*Gorr.* "I've no idea what you're talking about."

"Is it a male I know?"

Annora sighed. "No."

"I don't believe you. Who?"

"No one."

Nayla made an amused sound. "You also have a massive but sexy bruise on your neck."

Annora automatically touched it. *By fangs and claws.*

Her sister looked highly amused. "I wanted to see if you were free for breakfast."

"I'd love that, Nay, but I have work."

Her sister's pretty face turned serious. "The Sarkans."

"Yes."

Nayla turned to look at the trees, lost in thought.

"Hey." Annora touched her sister's arm. "You okay?"

Nayla had been held captive by Candela. It wasn't an experience you forgot quickly...as Thadd knew.

She shot Annora a small smile. "I am. I'm not exactly over it, but even when I was terrified, I knew my awesome, kickass sister would find me."

Annora tugged Nayla in for a hug. She loved her sister so much. "Always." She was just sorry it had taken her so long to find and free Nayla and her friends.

"Yes, and you and that hunky Zhalton—" Nayla broke off, her eyes going wide. "By the claws, that's whose scent you're covered in. He left that mark."

Annora growled. "Nayla—"

Her sister grinned, looking giddy. "I *love* this. He's big and bossy and strong. You've never found anyone who didn't wither under the infamous Annora Rahl glare."

"I need to get to work." She tried the glare, but Nayla was immune, as well. "Are you done?"

"For now. Thadd 'ruggedly handsome' Naveri. *Perfect.*"

"I'm not confirming anything. Go." Annora shooed her. "I don't have time for interfering little sisters."

Nayla laughed, then met Annora's gaze. "I love you, Nora."

Her heart melted. "I love you too, Nay-bug."

"I want you happy. You deserve that." With a wave, Nayla skipped down the path.

Annora opened her door. Work. She needed to get to work.

She loved her cabin. Inside, she kept her decorating minimal, except for pops of rich colors—blue, red, green —against the wood. Her small kitchen with black stone counters didn't get used much, but she loved it. A comfy couch in a deep beige sat in front of her fireplace.

In her spacious bedroom, dominated by her carved, wooden bed, she stripped off her clothes and headed for the shower. The shower stall was lined with river rocks, with a huge showerhead on the ceiling. Showering in it made her feel like she was in the rain.

Or under a waterfall.

At the reminder, desire flickered in her belly.

She turned the water to cold.

It didn't take Annora long to wash, and slap on some lotion. She studied the bruise on her neck in the mirror and felt a flash of something. A little part of her didn't mind that mark all that much.

She didn't cover it up. Damari were used to seeing the evidence of passion, and she'd just have to dodge the nosy questions.

She pulled on some supple, leather pants, a blue

111

shirt, and boots. Once she was ready, she headed out to Brodin's cabin.

The wood-and-glass cabin sat at the top of a rise. It had a sharply pitched A-frame roof, and was made of deep red wood. She knocked on the door, and a moment later, her emperor opened it.

"Annora."

"Brodin." She eyed him. "You look disgruntled."

He made a harrumphing sound. "My mate spent the night hunched over her comp, muttering, instead of in our bed."

"Ah." Annora followed him in. "Did she make any progress?"

"I think so, but her liberal cursing makes it hard to tell." Brodin paused, his gaze zeroing in on Annora.

It took everything she had to stand still and not let her face change. "What?"

"You look... Different."

Brodin was extremely observant. She cleared her throat. "Black hair, brown eyes, tall. Same as always."

"You're more relaxed than usual." His gaze snagged on her neck. "Ah."

She made a sound. "You really want to discuss our sex lives?"

"I'm a mated man. I'm not that interesting anymore. But my lovely, choosy First Claw on the other hand..."

"Drop it, Brodin." She strode past him.

The large, open living area was done in warm, rich wood and a large, dominating stone fireplace rose all the way up to a high ceiling that was crisscrossed with wooden beams. Huge couches faced the fireplace. She and the other cleavers had spent many an evening sprawled on those couches.

On the wooden mantel was a row of small, metal mechanica. The tiny devices were all different—children, wolves, dancers, warriors. Poppy liked making them.

Annora found Poppy at the long, wooden table. She had a Damari comp in front of her, her fingers moving fast. Her blonde hair was disheveled, and she was gnawing on her bottom lip.

"Poppy?" Annora said.

"What?" There was a deep groove in the woman's brow. She blinked, looking like a baby hellie bird. "What is it?"

"I'm wondering if you've decoded the data?"

"Annora?" Poppy blinked. "Where did you come from?"

Annora fought a smile. Poppy often got lost in her work. "I just arrived."

"Are you all right? After the mission to Andret?"

"Fine. But we need to find that genite shipment."

"I know." Poppy tiredly rubbed her temple. "I've gotten through some layers. Arteen from the science team helped."

"The man fell asleep a few hours ago," Brodin muttered.

"I just need—" The comp chimed. Poppy leaped on it like a starving wolf sensing roasted meat. "I... Oh. Well." She beamed, the tiredness dropping from her face. "I'm in!"

"Really?" Annora smiled.

"Really."

"My clever mate." Brodin cupped Poppy's jaw, tilted her face, and kissed her.

Annora looked away, feeling a flash of envy. The pair was so in love, so in sync, as only mates could be.

"Okay." Poppy swiped the screen. "I found it. The genite was sent to somewhere called Abiosis."

Annora and Brodin cursed.

Poppy frowned. "Not good?"

"It's a space station," Brodin said. "A scientific space station orbiting Sarkan."

Annora gritted her teeth. "It's Naberius' domain."

---

THADD SNUCK into the guest cabin that had been assigned to him.

His bag was resting on the neatly made and un-slept-in bed. Instantly, he thought of waking alone in the scout hide this morning.

He was unsurprised that Annora had snuck out on him. His mind filled with memories of the night, and all the other things they'd done on those furs.

He still smelled her, tasted her...

Shaking his head, he strode into the bathroom, stripping off the clothes he'd borrowed from the stash in the hide. He'd climbed the waterfall, which had proven to be good exercise to clear his head. He'd retrieved both his and Annora's discarded clothes.

Turning on the shower, he caught his reflection in the mirror.

His lips quirked. He was covered in scratches. He

turned to look at his back. It had been stinging all the way back to the city, and he saw why. His gorgeous wolf had left some deep claw marks.

He liked it, more than he should.

Thadd quickly showered and dressed in fresh clothes —black pants and a high-necked, black shirt.

There was a knock at the door.

He opened it to reveal a familiar cleaver. "Tolf."

"Hey, Thadd. Sleep well?" The man's silver hair gleamed in the morning light.

"Yes. The Damar air must agree with me."

As did being wrapped around Annora's sleek body.

"There's no cleaner air in the system," Tolf said. "We're meeting at the cleaver lodge. Poppy decoded the data."

Thadd straightened. "She found the location of the genite shipment?"

Tolf nodded. "See you soon."

Quickly, Thadd pulled on his boots and headed out to the low, wooden building the cleavers used. There was a training area attached to it, and he saw several Damari sparring.

He jogged up the front steps, eager to find the genite.

And eager to see Annora.

The group sat at a long table. He spotted Brodin first, the man's silver-gray hair pulled back at the base of his neck. He stood behind Poppy, who was seated in a chair at the table, working on a comp.

Like he sensed her, Thadd turned his head. Annora strode through the lodge. Her hair was in a ponytail, swinging behind her, and she was in clean clothes.

Her gaze met his. For one electric second, he saw something in them, then she pasted on her tough First Claw face. She nodded at him.

Like they were polite strangers, not like he'd had his cock deep inside her hours ago and she'd been screaming his name.

His hand curled into a fist.

"Thadd," Brodin said. "I hope you're well rested, because we have another mission for you."

"I slept very well. My bed was very comfortable."

"Good." Brodin waved a hand at the table. "Take a seat."

The table was loaded with platters of food. Thadd filled a plate.

"You decoded the data, Poppy?" he asked.

The woman from Earth nodded. She looked tired, with dark circles under her eyes.

"It took me a while." A faint smile. "But I got it."

Brodin stroked a hand down her back. "I never doubted it."

Her comp chimed. "I have calls coming in from Zhalto and Taln."

Projections speared up above the table. On one side, it showed Graylan, and on the other side, Rhain's face appeared.

Thadd's overlord caught his gaze and nodded. Thadd nodded back.

"Rhain, Graylan," Brodin said. "Poppy decoded the data."

"Well done, Poppy," Rhain said.

Graylan nodded. "Where's the genite?"

Poppy sucked in a breath. "It's been sent to Abiosis."

Thadd frowned. The name sounded familiar.

"It's a space station in high orbit around Sarkan," Brodin said.

Thadd cursed. The two kings on the screen cursed as well.

"You've heard of it?" Annora asked.

"We have some unsubstantiated intel about a space station," Thadd said.

"Naberius works off Abiosis," Annora said.

Thadd's jaw tightened.

"It's Naberius' private playground." Graylan's eyes flashed. "Zavir set up the space station and his Zhylaw warlords have free rein. It's filled with labs."

"Do you have additional intel on it?" Brodin asked.

The conqueror nodded. "Bits and pieces. It has a dome area on top filled with vegetation. They grow all kinds of deadly plants for use in their research." He said the words in a scathing tone. "Beneath the dome is the bulk of the station. Labs, cells, living quarters for the scientists."

"So we go to Abiosis and destroy the genite." Thadd crossed his arms over his chest. "And if we destroy Naberius at the same time, we'll be doing the entire system a favor."

"It's not as easy as that, Captain," Graylan said. "Abiosis is rumored to have high-level security. Just getting aboard is near impossible. It is regularly patrolled, and all entrances are heavily shielded."

Annora sucked in a breath. "So we need proper authority to enter."

Graylan gave a short nod. "Or you sneak aboard undetected."

Thadd frowned. "Is that possible?"

"My obsidian team—" Thadd knew that was Graylan's elite team of fighters "—has speculated that a small stealth ship could make it through the patrols. They've identified several exhaust ports on the space station that are not shielded." The conqueror raked a hand through his hair. "I'll transmit the data. It's all speculation. It might not work, and we have limited knowledge of the inside of the space station."

"Your Highness," Annora said. "We believe that Naberius got off Andret. If he's on Abiosis with the genite..."

Graylan's mouth flattened. They all knew what that meant.

"I'll get aboard," Thadd said. "I'll destroy the genite."

"Thadd." Rhain's tone was deep, concerned.

Thadd met Rhain's gaze. "The Zhylaw cannot be permitted to use the genite. I won't let them torture the Talnians."

Annora shot to her feet, facing him. "You can't go alone."

"I can. It'll be easier for one person to sneak in—"

"Easier to get caught and killed." Her hot gaze bored into his.

"It would be best if I go alone," he growled.

She sniffed. "I'm Damari, Captain, so growling doesn't intimidate me. And it would be better if you had someone to watch your back. I think the destruction of the mining camp proved that there is merit to working as a *team*, rather than a lone and surly hero of one."

Someone at the table made a choked sound, but Thadd didn't turn to look.

His and Annora's gazes clashed. They stared at each other, and he willed her to back down.

But of course, the hardheaded Damari didn't. She held his gaze and crossed her toned arms.

Someone cleared their throat and Thadd managed to pull his gaze off her. He looked back at the amused kings —the two on the screen, and the one in the room.

Graylan cleared his throat again. "Our starships are equipped with a small, experimental stealth spy ship that has superior masking technology. Vash and Hagen can explain it. If you take the stealth ship, which only fits two people, you should be able to sneak into the space station." His lean face hardened. "But it's a dangerous mission. If you're caught..."

Thadd tried to ignore the cold sweat that broke out on the back of his neck. He'd be back in Zhylaw hands, right in the heart of their labs.

Suddenly, he felt a brush on his thigh.

The faintest touch of Annora's fingers. She didn't look at him, but her touch steadied him.

"I can't ask you to do this," Graylan said.

"You don't have to," Annora replied.

Thadd nodded, accepting that Annora wouldn't back down. "We volunteer."

Emotion crossed the conqueror's face. "Why?"

"Because it's the right and honorable thing to do," Thadd said.

"And our planets can only defeat Zavir if we work together," Annora added.

Thadd saw pride on Rhain and Brodin's faces.

"Thank you," Graylan said. "I'll have my people transfer what information we have on the Abiosis space station to the stealth ship. We have a saying on Taln. May your path be smooth and your sky clear. Good luck to both of you."

# CHAPTER TEN

Annora was back in the elevator, heading to the landing pads. She wore a new spacesuit and she was ready.

She'd stopped by to visit her parents and Nayla. They hadn't hidden their worry, but they knew she was dedicated to her job. Nayla had given her a cute charm on a chain for luck. Made of silver, it featured wolf claws crossed with a sword. Her sister wasn't very subtle.

Her mother had pulled her aside before she'd left. *You don't always have to push yourself so hard, my lovely girl. You have nothing to prove, and you don't always have to hide your softer side. You have a loving heart.*

The elevator slowed and the doors opened.

The first thing she saw was Thadd.

His black spacesuit slicked over that magnificent body of his. His hard abs were clearly on display through the fabric.

Abs she'd licked.

*Gorr.* Maybe she wasn't quite as ready as she thought.

She needed to stop thinking of the Zhalton's body and focus on infiltrating an enemy space station.

He turned and looked at her. He took in her suit before nodding. He was every inch the stoic Zhalton warrior. There was no sign of the man who'd groaned her name during their night together.

Gritting her teeth, she strode forward. Now, she noticed the small, sleek ship resting on the landing pad beside the larger Talnian ship they'd taken to Andret.

Yes, something was really wrong with her that she was so focused on Thadd that she'd missed the sexy, black stealth ship.

Its lines said it was clearly Talnian. It was a two-seater, with one seat at the front of the tapered nose, and one behind. There was a small cargo area at the back.

This ship was built purely for stealth, and didn't pretend otherwise. It had small, sleek wings that angled up and back.

She stopped beside Thadd. Vash and Hagen were nearby, circling the ship and checking it over. Vash consulted her comp pad, muttering to herself.

"Ready?" Annora asked.

"Ready. Are you sure you don't want to reconsider?"

"Don't make me mad, Naveri."

He grunted.

"Right." Hagen smiled at them. "You're going to love the Valiant. It is a sweet, fast ride."

The cockpit canopy was retracted back. The pilot leaned in, giving them a quick lesson on the controls.

"But don't worry," Vash said. "The ship's system can fly itself. It won't need much input from the two of you.

She also has state-of-the-art maintenance systems, so the ship can self-diagnose and repair most things."

That was good. "And the stealth capability will get us past Sarkan security?"

"It's the best in the system." Vash shrugged. "There are no guarantees. I hear the Sarkans protect that space station like a pack of rabid rock hounds."

Some animal from Taln, Annora guessed.

"She'll get you there." Hagen patted the black metal.

"Good luck." Vash's round face turned serious. "To both of you. All of Taln appreciates you doing this."

Annora nodded. "We'll see you when we get back."

She settled into the front seat, and Thadd sat in the seat behind her. The cockpit canopy slid over them. It was a smoky black.

The Talnian pilots waved.

Annora touched the console and lights lit up in sequence under her fingers.

"Take off sequence initiated," a pleasant female voice said.

The engines rumbled soundlessly to life, and she felt the faint vibration beneath her.

"Ready, Captain?"

"Always, First Claw."

Funny how she didn't mind him at her back now. How she trusted him to watch it.

And fight beside her.

The ship shot forward and into the air. She was pushed back into the seat. They picked up speed, soaring into the sky and she laughed. Oh, it was fast.

"Not a bad ride," she said.

"No complaints from me."

She knew him well enough now to read his tone. He was enjoying it.

They shot higher. Out the smoky window, she looked down. She saw the forest, dotted with lakes, and in the distance, the jewel-blue waters of the Duranti sea.

Then, they left Damar behind and hit space.

Ahead was vast black, dotted with bright stars.

A part of it amazed her, but she was a wolf at heart. A creature of the soil and trees. She liked her feet—and paws—on the ground.

But she'd do what needed to be done to destroy the genite.

Once the ship evened out and settled on the flight path, she pressed the button and her seat rotated to face Thadd.

He dominated the Talnian seat. Like some king on a throne.

"We should go over our plan," she said.

He nodded.

She touched the controls on the side of the console, and a projection appeared between them, showing the Abiosis space station based off Talnian intel.

It was an amazing piece of engineering, with a large dome on the top and the body beneath it like an iceberg.

"We head for the exhaust vent here." A gold spot appeared on the body of the space station, a few levels below the dome. "The Talnians said it's not as well protected. It's where the Sarkans vent stale air out of the dome. They depend on security patrols around the station to not allow anyone close enough to reach the vents."

"But the stealth ship should get us in undetected," Thadd said.

"That's the plan." She cocked her head, noting the grooves beside his mouth. She ran her tongue over her teeth. "We aren't going to end up in Zhylaw hands, Thadd. I won't allow it."

Those blue eyes, brilliant and glowing, met hers. "I'm fine."

"That word again. You're not. It's okay to have hang-ups about what you experienced. That makes you normal."

He scowled. He may as well have held up a sign that said off-limits.

Annora focused on the projection of the space station.

"Once we reach the vents?" he prompted.

She traced a path upward. "We don't have detailed schematics of the inside. We'll have to find our own way up to the dome. Based off what we do have, there are lots of species being kept in the dome." Her nose wrinkled. "We know Naberius likes to experiment. I assume his lab won't be too far away from the dome."

Thadd's hands gripped the armrests. "Okay. Get to the dome undetected, do some recon, find Naberius' lab and the genite."

She nodded. "Blow up the genite. Talnian intel says we can't get conventional explosives aboard the stations. The detectors will pick it up."

He gave a thin smile. "Which is why we're carrying Zhalton explosives. Until I charge them, they're inert."

"And you're sure you can charge them?" She remembered his pain on Andret.

He gave a clipped nod. "It won't be a problem."

Annora wasn't entirely sure she believed him. "Can you charge them without hurting yourself?"

"It will be fine."

*Ugh*. Men. "Thadd—"

"My abilities...have changed recently. I'm able to access energy in more locations and more easily than before."

Since he'd been hurt by Krastin. He sounded like each word was ripped from him. Annora stilled. If she was reading him right, he hadn't told anyone. "You're all right? It's not hurting you?"

He gave one curt shake of his head.

She kept her tone business-like. "Okay, well, you know your abilities better than anyone. So, we just need to get to the space station undetected." She checked the console. "We'll activate stealth mode in one ship hour. It uses a lot of power, but I want to be undetectable well before we're in visual range."

He nodded.

She noted how tense he was, his shoulders taut. It was a wonder he didn't snap in half.

She took a second to set a timer for the stealth mode. Then she looked back and saw that Thadd's knuckles were white from how hard he was gripping the armrests.

"Thadd?"

He looked at her and she sucked in a breath.

His blue eyes were boiling, edgy and deadly.

"Talk to me," she said quietly.

He stayed silent.

She unclipped her harness. There wasn't much room to maneuver, but she crouched in front of him.

"Get back in your seat." His voice was a gritty growl. If he'd been Damari, she'd think he was fighting to control his wolf.

"You shouldn't have come, if going into Sarkan territory gets to you this much."

"It's not that." He stared past her, out the cockpit canopy.

His neck muscles were so tight. She wanted to stroke his skin, soothe him.

*He is not yours, Annora. You have no claim on him.*

But when he closed his eyes, looking so tense he might implode, she tossed her caution aside.

Last night, he had belonged to her. She'd touched every part of him, let him have her.

She rose and straddled him. His eyes snapped open. She smoothed her hands up his arms, across his shoulders, and dug her fingers into his tense muscles, kneading.

"Annora." It was definitely a growl now.

"I'm being nice to you." She leaned down and kissed his jaw. "You need to get used to it." She peppered kisses along the stubborn, rugged line of his jaw. "And you're going to tell me what's bothering you. I need you focused."

He bumped his hips up, rubbing the bulge in his suit between her legs. She almost moaned.

"It's hard to be focused with you touching me." He

127

gripped her ponytail, and tugged her head back. Then his mouth was on hers—hard, possessive.

Instead of fighting it, she sank into the kiss. Soon, she cupped his cheeks, her tongue fighting against his.

*By the claws.* They broke apart, their foreheads pressed together. His big body was a little more relaxed beneath hers. Or at least, it was filled with a different, healthier kind of tension.

This strong man who lived for his duty, was a warrior. He hated showing weakness and kept his walls up to everyone around him.

"I hate the idea of taking you in there." He blew out a harsh breath. "Right into the heart of Zhylaw depravity and horror. If they touch you…"

Realization burst. He was worried about *her.* That his nightmare would become hers.

*Gorr.* He kept his walls up, but he'd let her in.

"Then I get to use my claws." She let them form, and pricked his neck before she bit his lip. "I like using them."

That earned her the faintest, faintest smile. "I know. I have the scratch marks to prove it."

"Please activate stealth mode," the console chimed.

*Time to focus back on the mission.*

With one last kiss to his lips, she sat back in her seat. It swiveled her back to the front.

Annora realized that she didn't want Thadd to put up his walls.

She just had to decide if she wanted to be the woman who didn't let him.

THADD STARED out the cockpit as the space station loomed above them.

It was impressive.

He might detest the Sarkans and the Zhylaw, but the space station was like a city floating in space. The dome on top gleamed. Inside, he could see dense green foliage, dotted with pops of brilliant color—red, purple, blue.

The lower levels almost dripped down from below the dome, punctuated by glowing windows.

He wondered what horrors lived inside.

Beyond the space station, the planet of Sarkan was visible.

It was a dark orb that glittered with orderly circles of lights. Almost all the planet was covered in dense cities.

There was also a lot of starship traffic. Large cruisers were heading to the surface. Smaller vessels came and went from the space station.

Tension filled the small ship. A part of him was waiting for space station security to discover them.

"The stealth tech is holding," Annora said.

She was tense too, monitoring the console, and also staring up at the space station.

A low alarm chimed.

"*Gorr*, a space station security ship is on an intercept path." She touched the controls. "Hold on."

The ship turned on its side and dived downward.

Thadd spotted the security ship. It gleamed a shiny silver, with a slim body and large, circular engines on the sides.

Had it detected them? His chest tightened. He

wished he had his sword in hand. Not that it would help in this situation.

But the security ship never slowed. It flew right past them, and Thadd let out a breath.

"Looks like they were just on a regular patrol." Annora adjusted their controls. Their ship zoomed upward. "There's the vent."

He saw the shadow of the large vent. It was just large enough for their ship to enter.

The stealth ship automatically slowed and flew them in. It tilted, nose down, and attached to the side of the wall inside the vent tunnel. Their seats tilted to keep them upright.

They were in.

"There's the panel we can use to access the station." She pointed just beyond the ship.

It was set into the wall. He nodded.

They activated their helmets and strapped on their weapons. The cockpit canopy retracted.

Annora unclipped, then leaped out of her seat. She floated over to the access panel.

There was a faint clunk as the grav-weights in her suit hit the wall. She hung there and waved him over.

Thadd pushed out of the ship and followed.

He both loved and hated the weightless feeling of space. It felt free, but he depended on his training, which he did with his feet firmly on the ground.

He hit the wall beside Annora and his grav-weights activated. She pulled out a small tool.

A glowing flame appeared as she used the torch to cut the bolts off the access panel. It swung open.

They climbed inside and he closed it behind them. They were in the small maintenance space between the inner and outer walls of the space station. It had a faint atmosphere.

She pointed and opened the door hatch into the space station. It hissed with the release of air pressure.

They entered into a dark corridor, closed the hatch, and retracted their helmets.

It was silent inside. The station had sleek, brown metal walls, and lights glowed along the base of them. The floor was a shiny silver, reflecting back their images.

"Let's go. We need to find a way up," Annora said.

And avoid any Sarkan or Zhylaw.

They moved silently down the wide hall. Lights blinked on along the floor. There were lots of closed doors, but Thadd didn't detect any energy inside. One door was open, and he peered in through the archway.

"Looks like personal quarters," he said, taking in the bed and desk built into the walls.

They came out in a larger, open area. There were some potted plants dotted around in circular containers, and an escalator headed up to the next level, flanked by curved, clear railings.

Thadd started to move, but Annora grabbed his arm.

They both flattened against the wall.

A second later, two Sarkans—a man and a woman— came out of the doorway. They were talking quietly to each other, and looking at a comp pad.

Scientists or workers. They didn't look around and passed by quickly.

"Go," Annora murmured.

They hit the escalator and the belt flared to life, moving them upward.

Thadd was tense, he felt exposed. If someone spotted them...

"I smell vegetation," Annora said.

They were getting close.

At the top of the escalator was another open area, this one dotted with green chairs attached to the floor. A large window gave a view of space and Sarkan. Although no one was sitting around enjoying it.

Thadd and Annora darted through the chairs.

"That way." She pointed. "The scent's stronger."

Thadd felt a trickle of energy. It felt...strange. "Wait."

"What?" Then she frowned. "I hear something coming."

They ducked down behind the plush chairs. They pressed close together and he slid an arm around her.

There was a faint, whirring noise.

They peeked over the chair.

A robot floated into view.

It had a roughly-triangular-shaped body made of gray metal. It was larger on top, tapering to a pointed bottom. A band of light rimmed the top of it.

It stopped, and a wall of blue light speared out from it.

It was scanning.

"Down." He yanked her to the floor and pressed his mouth to her ear. "It's some sort of security bot."

*Gorr.* If it detected them...

The robot moved closer, swiveling. It must've sensed something, but not enough to trigger its protocols.

Annora's fingers bit into his forearm as they waited, tense.

A moment later, the security bot's scan shut off. It swiveled and floated away.

"By the wolves." Annora released a breath. "That was close."

Thadd rose, pulling her up. "Let's get to the dome."

They stuck close to the wall, jogging down another corridor.

A faint scream echoed from somewhere.

Someone in pain.

His footsteps slowed.

"Hey." She gripped his arms, stepping in front of him. "You aren't alone."

He sucked in a breath. "I know."

"I'm here."

He nodded. "Let's just get to the dome and find the genite."

She cupped his cheek, then turned. They headed toward the large door at the end of the corridor.

When they reached it, the door opened automatically, with a faint hiss.

He wasn't Damari, but the scent still hit him—lush vegetation, rotting debris, the smells of animals.

Blood.

They stepped into the dome.

The glass gleamed overhead, but inside was a tangle of bushes, trees, and vines.

A bush nearby was laden with huge, purple blossoms the size of his head.

"I detest the people who created this, but it is beautiful." Annora stepped close to the foliage. "Let's find the genite."

They found a narrow path leading through the vegetation.

"Don't touch anything," she warned.

He stayed right behind her. He watched monkey-like creatures in the trees, leaping from branch to branch.

Thadd brushed past a vine. Suddenly, it snapped out and wrapped around his arm.

*Gorr.* He pulled, but the vine tightened. More of it curled around his arm.

A yellow, bell-shaped flower unfurled right near his face.

There was a flash of a knife. Annora sliced the head of the flower off, and it hit the ground with a dull thwap. Then she cut through the vines holding his arm.

He stepped back, rubbing his wrist.

"A cralla from Damar," she said. "They immobilize their prey, then spray them with a toxin." She kicked the flower.

"Nice."

She smiled. "We like it wild on Damar."

"I know."

They shared a look, and in that instant, they were both thinking about sex.

He cleared his throat. "Can you sense any life forms? There's too much interference for my senses."

She nodded. "This way."

They passed through a narrow stream. She held up a hand.

Voices echoed nearby.

"Move it," someone snapped. It was a Sarkan accent.

Carefully, Thadd and Annora crouched and pushed some large leaves aside. They spotted Sarkan guards leading a line of pale-brown, fur-covered beings who walked upright on two legs through the dome. The beings were all chained together.

"Sharquoks," Annora said. "Their planet is in the neighboring system."

"Move faster." A guard shoved one Sharquok, and the being stumbled. A bright line of blue-green colored fur on the top of his head indicated he was male.

The Sharquoks were all painfully thin. So much so that their ribs were sticking out. They were in bad condition.

Anger pulsed through Thadd, and his hands fisted. He wanted to charge out there and free them.

Annora's hand closed over his, and he managed to breathe.

"Naberius is waiting for these ones," a guard at the back of the line called to the other. "He won't like it if we're late."

"Move!" the first guard yelled.

The group disappeared into the greenery.

"Okay?" Annora whispered.

Thadd nodded.

Her jaw tightened. "We can follow them to Naberius."

# CHAPTER ELEVEN

Annora moved silently and cautiously down the path the guards and prisoners had taken.

A screech echoed through the trees, followed by a long howl. The sound seemed to fill the dome. She stilled.

A predator had just made a kill.

Thadd touched her shoulder. They kept moving, pushing aside vines and low-hanging branches.

There was no sign of the prisoners.

She narrowed her gaze, and scanned the surroundings. All her senses were on high alert. Something felt off.

"What is it?" Thadd murmured.

"I don't know."

There was no movement. No signs of animals.

*Wait.* It was silent. There were no noises close by.

She gripped his arm. "Something's wrong."

A fierce scowl creased his brow.

She tugged him sideways. They needed to get away. Now.

Ahead was a strange tree with turquoise fronds and large, bulbous, orange fruit growing near the trunk. A pungent scent came from one of the other plants and clogged her nostrils.

She stepped into a clearing, muscles tense.

Thadd grabbed her wrist and squeezed. "I sense energy signatures."

"How many?" she asked.

He shot her a frustrated look and shook his head. "I can't tell. I can't even tell what they are."

Was it animals? Prisoners? Guards?

Suddenly, there was a whirring noise overhead. They both froze and looked up. Several spherical drones flew over the dome in formation. They paused, opened their bellies, and water poured down from them like rain.

*Gorr.* It must be how they watered the plant life in the dome.

Visibility turned to nothing. The water ran down their suits and drenched their hair. Annora felt it trickle down the back of her collar.

Around them, the ground turned to mush. Mud sucked at her boots.

Thadd jerked his head and pushed the vines aside. They kept moving, but she could barely see anything.

Anyone could attack and she wouldn't see them coming. She gritted her teeth and kept walking. At least the artificial rain wasn't cold. In fact, the humidity was rising.

"Fuck," Thadd muttered, wiping his face.

"Earth is rubbing off on you."

"Mal uses it a lot in training."

His tone was warm. "You like her."

"Yeah. I was wary of her at first. I thought she was a Sarkan trap set for Rhain. She's reckless, but brave, and she loves him."

"It was the same story with Poppy. Brodin was enthralled right from the beginning. I resented it, but she's smart, frighteningly courageous even though she's not a warrior, and she loves Brodin to distraction."

The deluge increased. Thadd ducked under a long branch, and pulled Annora close.

They stood in their makeshift shelter and watched the rain fall. For a second, she was back at the waterfall with him.

She liked being with him. Far too much.

Finally, the rain started to decrease. She watched rivulets running down the trees and after a few minutes, they slowed to nothing.

The drones flew away, while water still dripped off branches, trees, and leaves.

"Okay, let's circle back—" she stepped out from under the branch "—and we can—"

Bodies leaped out of the trees. Annora reacted on instinct, spinning away.

The Sarkan guards landed, holding long batons. As they held them up, the ends lit up, crackling with white energy.

*No.* Gorr.

Thadd moved, drawing his sword in one fluid motion. He slashed, cutting at the nearest guard, and opening up the man's chest.

The guards surged closer.

More guards came out of the trees. There were twelve in total. Two security bots floated in, guns sliding out of the sleek, metal bodies.

"Surrender," a guard said, spinning his baton.

"Hmm, let me think... No." Annora turned to look at Thadd. "Ready?"

"Ready," he replied.

They both whirled and attacked.

The guards swung their batons, energy crackling. Annora ducked and punched, letting her claws slide free. She smiled. She slashed another guard and blood sprayed the muddy ground.

Her blood heated. She fell into the fight.

*Kick, slash, punch.* She lunged. A guard's baton flew at her, and she leaped up, jumping over it. She took two steps, jumped, and wrapped her legs around the guard's head.

He yelled, but she twisted and took him down. His baton hit the ground, sizzling against a pile of wet leaves.

She looked up. Thadd was fighting with pure strength, grit, and power.

A guard was sneaking up behind him.

"Thadd!" she yelled.

Like he read her mind, he swiveled and kicked the incoming guard. The man dropped his baton and flew backward into the bushes.

Vines moved like scavengers, wrapping around the thrashing man.

There was a whine of a laser. Annora felt a sting on her side. Cursing, she ducked.

"Annora!" Thadd bellowed.

She touched her side and saw blood on her fingers.

"It's just a graze." Through the bushes, she saw the security bots converging on them.

*Gorr.* She darted out and leaped, pulling her knife.

She sailed through the air and landed on top of one bot.

*Got you.* She raised her arm and rammed the knife into the top of it.

Sparks exploded. The bot bobbed drunkenly, and she leaped off. It crashed into the ground, mud splattering.

The other security bot flew straight at her. Annora gasped. There was no time to evade, no time to attack.

Suddenly, it stopped.

She turned her head and saw Thadd striding toward it, palm outstretched.

The bot whirred, then crumpled inward on itself.

She straightened. He was incredible.

A guard barreled out of the forest.

Thadd swiveled and threw out his hand.

The guard rose up off the ground, his legs kicking.

Annora saw the glow of gold energy on Thadd's hands. It whirled around his arm, covering his body. For a second, she saw a faint glow around him. Like ghostly wings made of gold and fire burning behind him.

*What the gorr?*

The guard flew up, and slammed into the branches above. There was a sharp crack of snapping bone.

Thadd released the man and he dropped fast. He hit the ground and didn't move.

"You okay?" Thadd strode toward her.

"Fine." She pushed her sodden hair out of her face. Her side stung but the shot hadn't hit anything vital.

He wrapped an arm around her. She took a second and leaned into him, absorbed some of his strength.

"They know we're here," he said darkly. "We need to move fast."

"All right. We can—"

A drone buzzed overhead. *Gorr*. More rain?

Faint spray filtered down. She felt it wet the skin on her cheeks.

Then it started to burn.

Thadd coughed. His skin flushing red.

"What is it?" she cried, coughing. Her throat and lungs burned.

"Some...chemical agent." His muscles strained and he groaned.

Annora could see holes being burned into her suit. She scratched at her arms. It hurt to breathe.

She stumbled and fell to her knees in the mud.

"Get up." He tried to pull her up.

But her lungs hurt too much. She heard voices. More guards spilled out of the trees.

"They're incapacitated," someone said.

Thadd staggered. He tried to fight the nearest guard, grabbing the man's baton.

Another guard rushed in. Annora's vision was blurry, and she couldn't seem to form the words to warn Thadd.

The guard landed a brutal blow to the back of Thadd's head.

He pitched forward and hit the mud.

*No.* She tried to crawl toward him. He wasn't moving.

The guard spun his baton and held it right in front of her face. "Don't move."

She quivered, helplessness mixing with her pain and anger.

"You were right where we were told you would be." Naberius nimbly stepped out of the trees.

Her heart sank. The *gorr*-cursed scum was smiling.

The warlord's skin looked even bluer than it had on Andret. His mechanical eye whirred as he looked at Thadd, then Annora.

"First Claw Rahl. I'm so pleased you could join us." Naberius rubbed his hands together. "I owe you for destroying my genite mine." The warlord's smile dissolved, a hard gleam appearing in his eye. "You'll regret it. I know a lot of painful things to do to a Damari body." He looked at Thadd. "And to Zhaltons."

Annora ground her teeth together. *No.* She would *not* let this man have Thadd. This was Thadd's worst nightmare. It would break him.

She managed to pull a breath into her burning lungs. No, Thadd would never bend or break.

"You knew we were coming?" she said slowly.

"Yes. I just had to give the right incentive to the right person."

"Who?" she barked. She couldn't begin to imagine who had betrayed them.

"A man named Hagen."

*No.* It felt like a blow to her chest. How could the

Talnian work with this monster who was out to destroy Taln? The pilot had been so friendly.

"The pilot has a young child with health needs," Naberius said. "The promise of wealth and a new home made him malleable."

She closed her eyes. It still stung, but she knew many parents would go to any lengths to save the life of a child. Gorr, she would as well.

Naberius crouched in front of her. This close, she saw how deep his burn scars were on his face. "I really, really want to strap you and the captain to a bench in my lab—"

Annora lunged.

The guard behind her hit her with a baton. She landed back on her knees, mud squelching beneath her.

"Unfortunately, my king has other ideas. Zavir thinks you're both too dangerous."

"Come closer and I'll show you," she growled.

Naberius laughed and rose. "I like your spirit. I wish I had time to break it." He shrugged. "No matter. I can't break you, but Krone will."

She stiffened. "Krone?"

"A secret moon of Sarkan. Our dumping ground. It's a real cesspool."

Annora's gut cramped.

"It's where we dump all our enemies, dissidents, and criminals." With a laugh, the warlord waved at the guards and strode away.

## THADD STIFLED A GROAN.

Pain radiated through his body. He made a quick self-assessment—he had no broken bones, no internal bleeding.

The hard surface beneath him was vibrating, and he opened his eyes.

He was in the empty cargo area of a ship. His ankles and wrists were chained to the floor. He felt the brush of fingers through his hair, and turned his head.

*Annora.* Thank the auroras.

She was chained to the floor beside him. While he was lying down, she was sitting up, her face pinched, her fingers stroking his hair.

Crushing dread hit him.

The space station. The Sarkan guards. He and Annora had been caught. They were in the *gorr*-cursed hands of Naberius.

The stroking fingers stopped. "Thadd?"

He looked up.

"Thank the wolves." She cupped his cheek. "You've been out for a while. "

"Are you all right?"

She nodded, but there was a bruise on her cheek and dried blood on her arm.

"I'm fine." She tapped his cheek. "And I do know the meaning of that word."

He tried to sit up, more aches and pains erupting. She helped him. They were alone in the echoing cargo hold.

He frowned. "Where the *gorr* are we?"

"On a ship."

Okay. This was better than being sliced open on a

bench in Naberius' lab. The Sarkans had clearly stripped them of their weapons and left them with nothing. For a second, he mourned the loss of his sword. He glanced at his forearm and his gut tightened. The Sarkans had even smashed up the comp units fitted into the suits.

Thadd grunted. "I figured the warlord would be cutting us open by now."

Her fingers entwined with his. "He was there, in the dome. I'm pretty sure he wanted to."

Thadd swallowed, then reminded himself that he wasn't alone. The fiercest fighter he knew was with him. And she was good motivation—he'd do anything to save her.

"We were sold out." Her voice was grim.

He frowned. "What?"

"Betrayed. By Hagen. Naberius knew we were coming."

Now Thadd sucked in a shocked breath. Hagen? How the *gorr* had the Talnian pilot fooled them?

"He did it to save his child." Her nose wrinkled. "It's not an excuse to sell out people trying to save your entire planet and people, but still..."

"It isn't the child's fault, but I will make sure Hagen pays. So many lives are at stake. So, why isn't Naberius sharpening his tools to make us bleed?" Thadd fought back his dark memories, ones that were coated in slick panic.

"Because Zavir figured we were too dangerous," she said.

That got a feral smile from Thadd. "Maybe Zavir isn't as dumb as I thought."

"We're en route to be dumped on a moon."

Thadd stiffened. "Krone?"

"That's it."

"*Gorr*." He thumped his fist on the metal floor. This was worse than Naberius' lab.

Annora studied his face. "I don't know much about Krone. The warlord said it was a dumping ground for Sarkan's enemies and prisoners."

"He wasn't lying. It's a dangerous, savage moon. The Sarkans don't let out much information about it. I've heard the Zhylaw also dump their failed experiments there."

Annora muttered a curse. "Atmosphere?"

"Breathable, but that's the only thing it has going for it. It's a desert moon. Rocky and desolate. There are no pretty dunes or oases. It's harsh and deadly. There can be sandstorms, rainstorms, high winds. The atmosphere is full of dust particles, so its sky is yellow."

"Sounds charming."

"There's no infrastructure, Annora. If they dump us there, there are no communications towers or space ports. There's no way off."

She gripped his hand tightly. "We'll be together, and we're dangerous, too. Brodin, Rhain, and Graylan will come for us."

Thadd pulled in a breath. "We may not survive Krone long enough for them to work out where we are."

"Ah, there's the grumpy captain I know so well."

"Annora—"

"I know your overprotectiveness is going into overdrive, but we've got this. You and me, together. I can finally get you to master this teamwork thing."

He couldn't stop himself. He leaned forward and captured her mouth.

She moaned and leaned into the kiss.

By the auroras, she tasted so good. They both pulled back, breathless.

And that's when he felt the ship slow.

"We must be getting close," Annora said.

Thadd steeled himself. He would do whatever it took to ensure Annora got off Krone alive. He would fight and kill, give his life... Whatever it took.

The vow steadied him.

Ignoring his throbbing headache and the aches in his body, he waited for the ship to land.

They felt when they hit the atmosphere. The ship shook wildly, and he and Annora were jerked against the chains holding them to the floor.

Then the ride evened out.

"We must be nearing the landing spot," he said.

"I hope so," she replied through gritted teeth.

But no guards appeared. Thadd frowned.

Suddenly, an alarm blared. The back ramp of the cargo bay started to open.

What the *gorr*?

Wind rushed in—hot, laden with sand. It washed over them as the ramp lowered.

The floor under them started to tilt.

His chains clanked, and he heard Annora cursing.

The floor continued to tip downward until it was

nearly vertical, and they found themselves dangling, the chains the only things holding them in place.

He looked down, wind and sand stinging his eyes.

Far below, he saw the rocky, desolate ground. It was all a washed-out yellow. They weren't very high up, but it was still a long drop.

What the *gorr* did the Sarkans think—?

There was a clank as their chains released.

"Thadd!"

He and Annora slid down the metal ramp, picking up speed.

*Gorr!*

Energy jolted through his system. He reached for Annora and grabbed her.

They fell out of the ship, and plummeted.

Sand and rock rose up to meet them.

Thadd yanked her closer, curling his body around hers. He reached for energy. Any energy. It was instinct.

And he found it.

It felt strong, laden with power.

He pulled it to him and let loose with a burst.

Their fall slowed a little. His skin prickled from the power.

Then they hit.

The air was knocked out of his lungs. He tasted sand.

"Ugh." Annora rolled onto her back.

Thadd did the same. More aches vibrated through his body.

They'd hit hard, and he had to work to pull air into his lungs. Overhead, he saw the Sarkan ship pull away. It flew into the faded yellow sky, turning into a gray speck, then disappeared.

Thadd rolled. "You okay?"

"I'll live." She winced and touched her side. "Thanks to whatever you did. You can access the energy here?"

He nodded. It shouldn't be this strong. He breathed deeply. But he finally had to accept the truth he'd tried to ignore since his captivity.

His abilities had changed. What the Zhylaw had done to him had altered him permanently. It wasn't fading, and his powers weren't going back to how they'd been before.

Thadd rose, and pulled Annora up. She dusted herself off.

"You want to talk about it?" she asked.

"Not really." He pulled in a breath. "Whatever Krastin did changed me. I have to accept that."

She was quiet for a moment. "It seems your powers are better now. Maybe it isn't a bad thing."

"Maybe." He wasn't sure anything good could come out of Krastin's torture.

"So," she said, scanning the bleak landscape.

It didn't look any better from down here.

Thin, sandy soil was punctuated by darker rocks. There was no vegetation. He turned in a circle. In one direction, he saw vague shadows that looked like blocky cliffs.

"We've got no food or water," she said, her tone no nonsense.

His lovely wolf wasn't afraid. She was facing the situation with a cool calm he admired.

"We'll need shelter, too." His gaze moved back to the cliffs.

She looked too, then glanced around. She stiffened. "Thadd."

He turned, and all his muscles went tight.

Huge, billowing clouds the color of deep, yellow-brown filled the sky behind them. Bright flashes of lightning forked within the haze.

"Sandstorm," he said.

"I'm guessing the winds will be strong," she said.

A muscle in his jaw worked. "The sand will be tough on the skin and eyes. Let's head for the cliffs."

She nodded.

He took her hand, squeezed. He really missed his sword.

But they weren't giving up.

They set off at a run.

# CHAPTER TWELVE

As they jogged across the rough, unforgiving landscape, Annora ignored the twinges in her body from the fall.

It would've been a lot worse if Thadd hadn't slowed them.

She glanced at him. He wasn't moving smoothly. He was in some pain, but the stubborn man wouldn't admit it.

The huge cliffs were clearer now. They rose above them, blocky and chunky. The dark mouths of several caves were visible high up the cliff face.

Then she glanced back behind them.

The massive sandstorm was gaining on them. The clouds—dense and frightening—billowed and churned.

The wind tugged at her hair, and sand began pinging off her exposed skin.

She leaped over a large rock, then tensed to leap another one just ahead. Then she realized it wasn't a rock.

She slowed.

It was the skeleton of some horrible beast, half buried in the sand. The bones were bleached white, and it was far larger than her, with three wicked horns on its head. It had had a powerful rib cage and serpentine body.

She hoped whatever species it was had died out centuries ago.

"Keep moving," Thadd said.

She nodded.

The ground started to get rockier, littered with large, rectangular boulders like a giant had tossed them. They'd clearly fallen from the cliff a long time ago.

She and Thadd dodged the boulders, picking up speed.

Visibility was dropping and the wind howled like a hungry beast searching for prey. Sand was a constant drum on her back, and getting in her eyes.

Then all of a sudden, Thadd grabbed her arm and jerked her to a stop.

"What is it?" She scanned around them. All she saw were rocks, and the decreasing visibility was making even those hard to see.

"I sense energy signatures," he said.

Tension filled her. "Where?" She couldn't see anything in the sand.

"All around us."

Annora frowned. There were only rocks.

Then she saw a shape rise up *out* of the sand.

*Oh,* gorr.

Several more rose.

Her Damari instincts flared. It was some sort of alien wolf-dog.

They were as high as her chest, with powerful, canine bodies covered with leathery, brown skin instead of fur. They sported only a ruff of ragged, brown fur around their necks.

One of the beasts growled. It had a pointed snout, filled with needle-like teeth, and long, pointed ears held straight up.

Their golden eyes gleamed, covered by a gleaming film.

The skin and film would give them perfect protection from the sand. They were well-adapted to Krone's environment. They must be some sort of native creature.

"Nice alien doggies," she murmured.

Thadd raised a brow. "We don't have time for this. The sandstorm will be here soon, and we need shelter."

The five wolf-dogs circled them.

"I don't think they care." She could change. Her wolf was as large as these animals.

But the shift would take time. They were poised and ready to attack. For a few seconds, she'd be helpless.

The lead dog, the largest of the pack, charged. Thadd dodged, then rammed his weight into the canine. It hit the sand on its side, its dangerous jaws snapping.

Another wolf-dog started toward Annora, growling. She kicked at it, hard. It leaped back, but was unhurt, just wary.

If the five attacked them at once, they'd tear Thadd and her to pieces. She really wished she had her club.

She needed a weapon.

She backed up, assessing. The wind picked up, tearing strands of her hair free from her hair tie.

Her foot hit something. She looked down and saw another horned skeleton buried in the sand.

A dog leaped. She dropped flat to the sand and it sailed over her. Nearby, another one leaped at Thadd. He gripped its jaws, holding it in the air. The muscles in his big arms strained.

He tossed the snarling wolf-dog aside.

Annora glanced at the rib cage of the skeleton, part buried in the sand. She touched the bones. They were strong, not brittle or too weathered. The ends looked sturdy, and the sides sharp.

She grabbed one and tried to snap it off.

It was too strong.

She rose and kicked it. It broke with a sharp snap. She kicked another one, and another. *Snap. Snap.*

She snatched up the longest rib bone.

"Thadd!" She threw it.

Like pure poetry, he turned and caught the makeshift weapon.

She saw him change his grip, test its weight, then he *moved*. He swung it like a sword at the incoming wolf-dog.

Thadd turned into a deadly whirlwind, the bone blade moving so fast it blurred. The alien wolf-dog yipped. It had a bloody gash on its side.

There was a low growl from behind her.

The wolf inside her bristled. Carefully, she grabbed the two other ribs that she'd kicked free.

She whirled and threw herself backward. She landed on her back on the sand, whipping the bone weapons up.

A large wolf-dog leaped at her. A second later, it impaled itself on her makeshift weapons.

Its heavy body sagged, hot blood splashing over her.

She heaved and shoved the animal off her. She leaped to her feet.

The other four alien wolf-dogs circled Thadd.

Her gaze narrowed. *Oh no, you don't.*

She ran. "Thadd!" She leaped.

He spun and slashed at a dog. She landed beside him, and they turned, their backs pressed together.

"Ready, Captain?"

"Always, First Claw."

They attacked. An alien wolf-dog snarled, and Annora snarled back.

She and Thadd moved together. She swung both her bone blades, and Thadd slashed with his larger one.

They moved with a synchronicity that stole her breath. She trained almost daily with her fellow cleavers, but she'd never had someone move like this with her. Anticipating her attacks, moving forward as she moved back.

She lunged low, and Thadd stabbed high.

She let her claws form, and slashed and stabbed at a wolf-dog, then spun. Thadd moved in fast to finish it off.

Two more alien dogs lay bleeding on the sand. The other two backed up.

The wind howled louder, and a huge gust hit them. It knocked Annora into Thadd. He steadied her.

She felt the wind scoring her cheeks. She blinked,

and saw the remaining two wolf-dogs were gone. They'd disappeared like they hadn't even been there.

"We need to get to shelter," Thadd yelled against the wind. He pointed.

She saw that the dense clouds were almost on them.

She nodded and her claws retracted. She slipped her bone weapons onto her back. Thadd did the same and they ran toward the cliff.

Annora dodged the rocky slabs on the ground. A huge gust of wind almost knocked her off her feet.

Thadd reached the rock wall first. It was lined with vertical cracks. He jammed his boots into one, reached up, and started to climb.

She braced herself and followed. Her focus narrowed to the climb, fighting to hold on and keep her balance with the wind tearing at her.

The openings to the caves were high above. They needed to reach one and hunker down.

She just hoped no other alien animals already called the caves home.

The wind picked up. A strong blast almost made her lose her grip. She clung to the wall for a second, then kept going. Her hair whipped around her face. There was so much sand flying around that she could barely see the rock right in front of her eyes.

She heard Thadd's curse. He was crossing a rough bit of the cliff face.

She gritted her teeth and continued up.

Suddenly, a powerful gust of wind rammed into her. Her hand slipped, her weight shifted.

Oh *gorr*, she was going to fall.

There was no time to scream.

But before she plummeted, a strong hand clamped onto her wrist. She looked up into Thadd's fierce face.

He slowly pulled her up. She gripped the wall again.

"Not far to go," he yelled.

She nodded.

They kept climbing. He stayed close, shielding her from the vicious wind with his big body.

Finally, after what felt like forever, they climbed over the edge onto a flat, rocky ledge.

Ahead, the rectangular mouth of a cave loomed, dark and menacing.

Thadd wrapped an arm around her, hauling her up, and they stumbled inside.

The wind cut off, and Annora let out a hard breath.

They were safe. For now.

THE WIND HOWLED past the cave entrance.

Heart pounding, Thadd gripped Annora's arms. "Are you hurt?"

"No." She swiped her hand over her face. Sand dusted her skin and suit. Then she reached up and ruffled his hair, and more sand flew everywhere.

"Come on, we need to get away from this cave mouth." He took her hand.

They moved deeper into the cave, which seemed to turn into a tunnel. It was mostly flat, with a few puddles of water. He wondered where they'd come from.

"There might be drinkable water somewhere in the cave system," she said.

He hoped so. His throat was as dry as the sand in his hair. As they continued, the light grew dim, but ahead, he saw a gold glow.

"Can you hear anything?" he asked.

"Only the wind."

"And I'm not detecting any energy signatures."

The tunnel joined up with others. The sound of the wind was more muffled now.

The golden glow intensified. They stepped into a junction, and they discovered veins of glittering gold rock in the walls that were giving off the light.

"Incredible." Annora stroked her hand over the glow stone.

They continued on, the glow stone lighting their way.

The tunnel opened into a small cavern. There was a hole in the ceiling overhead, and through it, they could see the sand clouds churning above.

"Thadd, look." Annora moved toward a wall. He walked over to join her, and blinked in surprise.

The walls were full of paintings of a tall people with lots of different animals.

"These are stunning," he murmured.

There were dozens of images, all over the walls, done in an array of colors. The paint looked old and weathered, but still held its vibrancy. There were people worshiping others on thrones. Pictures of cliffs and animals. People harvesting what looked like mushrooms in the caves. A naked woman bathing in a pool.

"A native species?" Annora suggested.

"It looks that way. Or maybe they were early Sarkans." He studied images of what looked like crops. "The climate must've changed. Perhaps after the Radiance."

"Yes. Look." She hurried to another wall. He saw someone had used white paint to color in the white flare, and beneath it, people cowered.

"It must've altered the landscape," Annora said.

"And this species died out. Let's keep going. We need to find water, and a place to rest."

She touched the front of her spacesuit. "And I want to wash off this animal blood."

The tunnel widened, and there were even more paintings.

They stepped into another cavern. Glow stone ringed it, giving it a soft luminosity.

A pool of water sat in the center, beautifully clear. Blue-and-white mosaic stones lined the bottom and edge of the pool.

"Beautiful," Annora said.

"I wonder if the water's drinkable."

"Only one way to find out." She knelt.

"Annora, no—"

She scooped up a palmful and drank. Her eyes warmed as she looked at him. "My Damari physiology can handle a mouthful of tainted water. Besides, this water is fine. I can't detect even the faintest trace of anything bad."

He released a breath. "It could have been deadly. I forbid you to—"

She rose, making an indelicate sound. "You what?"

Thadd pinched the bridge of his nose. Why couldn't he be drawn to a sweet, sensitive woman who didn't feel the need to run headlong into danger?

Because then he wouldn't be drawn to her.

"I don't want you hurt."

She smiled. "Then I'll let you off for that bossiness." She looked around and took another two steps. "Look." She walked into an adjoining room.

There were more mosaics, and Thadd noted three slender falls of water quietly landing into another pool.

"Mushrooms." She strode over to a patch of them growing by the base of the wall. They were brown and red and green, and came in lots of shapes and sizes.

"Like in the paintings." He glanced over them. "The locals were eating them."

"Great. I'm starving." She scooped up water from the pool and drank. Thadd crouched and did the same. It felt so good on his parched throat.

Annora plucked a red mushroom covered in white spots. "I'll test them out first." She gingerly nibbled the edge of it. Her eyes widened. "It's surprisingly good. Fleshy, and a little sweet."

He watched her carefully. "You feel all right?"

"They seem fine to eat."

They sat side-by-side, and ate and drank. The mushrooms weren't bad. Thadd sampled most of the different varieties.

Beyond the cavern, he could still hear the faint howl of the wind outside. The sandstorm continued to rage. He bit into another mushroom.

Annora suddenly rose. "I need to get clean."

Thadd stopped chewing.

She strode to the side pool with the waterfalls.

She touched the fastenings on her suit, and it fell off her. Beneath, she wore simple, black underwear that hugged her body. She discarded it as well.

And then she was gloriously naked.

Thadd drank her in. She was built so well, with long, toned legs, the subtle flare of her hips, her slim waist and firm breasts.

She unfastened her hair, and the long strands looked like black starfire.

She walked to the pool, giving him a perfect view of her ass. He was hard, his cock trapped by his suit.

When she glanced over her shoulder, she shot him a feminine smile.

She knew exactly what she was doing to him.

As she stepped into the pool, he scanned the area. There were no signs of any large life forms.

He rose and walked toward her. They'd survived this far. It still wasn't certain that they'd make it off this rock, but as long as they were alive and breathing, he'd fight.

For her.

For them.

Thadd unfastened his suit. He stepped out of it and his shorts.

Annora was under the waterfalls now, washing her hair.

She turned, saw him, and smiled.

Her dark gaze traced his body, over his chest, abs, then stopped at his rising cock.

"See something you like?" he asked.

"I do. Very much."

He stepped into the water. It was tepid—not hot or cold. He moved toward her.

The water only covered her up to her thighs.

She urged him under the small flow of water. Her hands moved over his chest, back, arms. She sifted her fingers through his hair, cleaning out the sand.

Then her fingers slid down his body. His muscles flexed as she circled his cock.

"Mmm, this I like very much," she said, pumping him. "More than I should."

"*Gorr*...Annora." Desire was like a bolt of energy to his gut. His cock swelled even more.

Then she dropped to her knees in the water.

She licked his abs, letting him feel the nip of her teeth. Thadd groaned.

"I like that sound," she purred.

"You like having me at your mercy," he countered.

She smiled up at him. "Yes."

What she didn't realize was that he was at her mercy all the time.

That he'd do anything for her. Fight for her, kill for her, die for her.

She gave his cock a squeeze, and nuzzled his thigh with her lips.

"Do it, Annora. Please." His voice was like grit.

She wrapped her mouth around the head of his cock.

He made an inarticulate sound.

She swallowed the length of him. He felt his cock slide deep into her welcoming mouth. The heat and suction made his legs weak. It was so good.

She moved up and down, her cheeks hollowing as she worked him.

Thadd slid a hand into her silky hair, trying not to explode.

She looked up at him, dark eyes glittering, her lips stretched around his cock.

He made another sound. He didn't want to come in her mouth. He needed to be inside her.

He pulled back and yanked her up.

"Thadd—"

He used his strength to lift her off her feet, following the driving need pounding inside him.

Annora automatically wrapped her legs around his hips, and gripped his shoulders.

"Your skin is so hot," she panted. "I feel the heat pumping off you."

He kissed her hard, tongue invading her mouth. He was pure need. A man who needed his woman.

He gripped her hips, shifted her, and thrust inside her.

Her cry echoed off the stone walls.

He stilled. Had he hurt her? She was hot and tight on his cock, and he could barely think.

"Move," she panted.

She felt so good, so right. Like a missing piece of himself.

He slammed into her.

She gripped his shoulders, using the leverage to ride him.

"Not...going to last," he said between gritted teeth.

"So don't." She bit the side of his neck, her hips moving, grinding against him. "Because I'm not."

She arched her back and came with a cry.

His wild wolf.

His own release hit, shuddering through his body. He gripped her hard and poured himself inside her.

## CHAPTER THIRTEEN

Annora woke up with her nose pressed against Thadd's neck, one leg tossed over his. She was mostly on top of him.

The warrior was providing her with something softer to lie on than the stone. Her heart squeezed. There was more to the man than he let people see.

The hard ground didn't seem to bother him. He was still asleep.

Annora realized that she no longer heard the roar of the wind outside. During the night, they'd rested, washed, and eaten, and enjoyed each other in several different ways. While they were wrapped up in each other, the sandstorm had passed.

Now it was time to find a way off this rock.

She shifted and kissed the side of Thadd's neck. His eyes opened instantly.

"Everything all right?" he rumbled.

"Yes." She pressed another kiss to him, surprisingly reluctant to let him go.

Her entire thirty-one years, she'd been perfectly fine to stand alone, to face down any challenge by herself.

Now, she was ridiculously grateful this man was with her.

*Gorr.* If anyone had told her this a week or two ago, she would've laughed so hard she would have pulled a muscle.

But here she was.

She kissed his neck again and sat up. "The sandstorm stopped."

When he didn't reply, she looked down.

He was staring at her breasts, lazy hunger stirring in his eyes.

They'd washed their suits and left them to dry, so they were both naked.

Annora cocked her head. "You spent plenty of time appreciating my...upper body during the night. It shouldn't generate that look in your eyes."

His fingers curled around her hip, and his gaze flicked up to hers. "It will always generate this look."

Warmth bloomed inside her. "Well, you'll have to save it for later. We need to do some recon—" she dragged in a breath, worry eating at her "—and see if we can find a way off this moon."

His face turned serious and he gave her hip a squeeze, then rose.

They washed, and pulled on their spacesuits, then filled up on mushrooms. After checking their bone weapons, it was time to go.

Annora cast one last glance around the grotto and the pools. Then she looked at Thadd.

He had his captain face in place—hard, a little grim. "Ready, Captain?"

His lips quirked. "Always, First Claw."

They headed out, moving fast and quietly through the tunnels. The glow stone was dull now, and it was much nicer without the howl of the sandstorm.

Light glowed at the end of the tunnel ahead—yellow and weak.

They stepped out onto the stone ledge.

Annora's chest locked. A desolate landscape spread out before them.

The sky above was a pale, washed-out yellow. The ground—a mix of sand and rock—was another shade of faded yellow. The rocks were a darker brown shade against the sand.

Other than that, there was nothing.

Like Thadd had said, there were no buildings, towers, or ships.

She lifted her chin. She was Annora Rahl. She was getting off this rock.

They still had the genite to deal with. Her jaw hardened. She was *not* letting Naberius get away with this.

She glanced at Thadd. Besides, she was yet to have Thadd naked in a bed.

She planned to do that.

"What's our plan?" he asked.

Since he was scanning the landscape, she didn't think he was thinking about sex right now. She saw the rock ledge they were on extended a long way along the cliff.

"Let's move along here on higher ground. See if we can spot anything."

With a nod, he set off first. They moved along the top of the cliff.

Periodically, Annora scanned around.

Rocks, sand, more rocks.

She spotted movement in the distance and stopped.

The vague shapes looked wispy in the hot vapor from the sand. It looked like a pack of the wolf-dogs they'd fought last night. She watched the powerful bodies loping across the barren landscape until they disappeared into the haze.

The sun rose higher in the sky, and the heat increased.

Since their spacesuits no longer had functioning controls, she was hot and sweating. She swiped an arm across her forehead.

With a growl, Thadd paused. He gripped the arms of his spacesuit and ripped them off, baring his muscular biceps.

"Come here." He gripped the arms of her suit and tore them off as well.

They kept going, the sun unrelenting. They'd need water before too long.

The rocky ledge grew rougher. Ahead, she saw long pillars of rock that had broken off from the main cliff. They stood tall, like sentries on duty.

Again, she swiped her arm across her forehead, then leaped onto the closest pillar, landing in a crouch.

"Annora," Thadd clipped out.

She turned and looked at his surly face.

By the claws, how had things come to pass that she now loved that grumpy look. "It's stable."

"It could've crumbled."

"But it didn't." She leaped onto the next one.

He grumbled, then jumped onto the first pillar.

They leaped across the pillars slowly, and she noted that each one was getting lower. They were like giant stepping stones taking them closer to the sandy ground.

They were almost at the bottom when she heard an animal howl.

She froze. Thadd landed beside her.

Another howl. Unhappy and afraid.

The sound of it echoed off the cliff face.

Thadd jerked his head. "That way," he murmured quietly.

They leaped down to the next pillar, and then onto the sand. They moved stealthily, and then she heard voices.

A deep drawl, followed by a high-pitched laugh.

Annora and Thadd crouched behind some large rocks as another howl, soaked with pain and fear, echoed around them.

Pulse drumming, she looked around the rock.

Three men in ragged clothes were tormenting an animal. Annora took it all in in seconds. One man poked the animal with a long, sharp spear made of stone.

The creature was about knee-high, with leathery skin and huge paws it hadn't grown into yet. The fur around its neck was just a fuzz.

A wolf-dog pup.

The men were lean, weathered. They had the hard edge of survivors. Their ragged clothes were ripped and stained.

169

"Let's cook the little gorr," one man said. "I haven't had meat in so long." He tossed back his bleached, blond hair.

Another man with long, matted black hair stabbed his spear at the pup.

The animal darted back.

The third man kicked at it. He was almost as wide as he was tall. He had four long tentacles coming from the back of his head and overlarge black eyes. His skin was a mottled gray-green. She hadn't seen his species before.

"I'm hungry," Tentacle man growled.

The wolf-dog pup cowered.

Beside her, she felt Thadd tense.

"I think we should intervene," he said.

She arched a brow. "So we can question these fine, upstanding men?"

"Yes," he replied, face serious.

"Not to rescue the pup?"

"That's just a happy by-product." Now he smiled, and it made heat curl in her belly. "And I feel like kicking some ass."

"Sounds like another of Mal's sayings. All right, Captain." Annora drew her bone blades. "After you."

---

BONE BLADE IN HAND, Thadd strode out toward the men. "Leave it alone."

The men all tensed and swiveled.

"Who the gorr are you?" Blondie asked.

"A newbie," the one with tentacles said in a gritty voice. "Can't have been here long, his suit's still shiny."

"It'll be three against one, newbie." The man with long, matted hair grinned, showing that his teeth were filed to sharp points. "It's not looking good for you."

"He's not alone." Annora stepped up on a rock beside him, her long body relaxed, her bone blades resting in her hands.

"A woman," Blondie breathed.

"A fresh, clean one," Tentacle added.

"A good-looking one," Matted Hair said. "She's mine first."

"Wow, you boys are so charming," Annora drawled. Her eyes flashed. "It'll be so satisfying to spray your blood all over the sand."

Blondie hooted, and Tentacle grinned.

"You'll be the one bleeding," Matted Hair replied.

Thadd ran out of patience.

He strode in and swung the bone at the gorr-sucking scum.

But these men hadn't survived here on Krone by being dumb or slow. Matted Hair swung his spear around and jabbed it at Thadd, lightning-fast.

Thadd whirled. The man came at him again and Thadd sidestepped. He thrust his bone blade at the man's arm.

It hit Matted Hair's elbow hard, and the bone in his arm broke with a crack.

Matted Hair roared.

Thadd followed by ramming the bone blade into the man's stomach.

The guy's mouth opened, closed, blood dripping down his chin.

Thadd yanked the bone blade back, then kicked the man. He flew backward and fell into the rocks.

With wild roars, the other two bandits charged.

Annora leaped off her rock, her bone blades slashing.

She cut at Blondie while Thadd faced the man with the tentacles. The man charged at Thadd, bellowing. Thadd shied right, ducked, and rammed his fist into the man's gut.

He spun and swung his blade, and wished he had his sword.

But the bone did the job. It sliced through the rags and cut into the man's side.

Out of the corner of his eye, Thadd saw Annora lunging and slashing, like a promise of death. Her opponent staggered back, barely keeping his feet, blood dripping onto the sand.

Thadd's opponent righted himself. He yanked a stone mace off his rope belt, clutching it in his hand. It was crudely carved.

"I'm gonna mess you up, newbie," Tentacle said.

Thadd just arched a brow.

The man was clearly too thick to see that he was losing. As Thadd watched, the man's tentacles changed color, showing his enhanced emotions.

"Then I'll stomp your dead body to mush. Then I'll take your woman and—"

"You going to talk me to death?" Thadd asked.

With a fierce shout, the man ran at Thadd, mace held high.

Thadd dropped and sliced his bone blade across the man's thigh. Blood spattered.

Tentacle went down, and their eyes met. Then Tentacle threw something at Thadd. He had no time to evade.

Whatever it was exploded in Thadd's face. Sand filled his eyes, nose, and mouth.

*Gorr.*

A heavy weight rammed into him. Through his blurred vision, he saw tentacle man right on top of him, then the guy clamped his beefy hands around Thadd's neck.

A stream of curses ran through Thadd's head. He tried to call energy to him, but he couldn't breathe, couldn't focus.

He heard a snarl.

The wolf-dog pup flew through the air and clamped its jaws on tentacle man's neck.

With a cry, Tentacle toppled off Thadd. Pushing up, Thadd sucked in air. He snatched up his bone blade and rammed it against the man's gut.

"Get...it off me," Tentacle choked out.

"Good dog," Thadd said. "Let him go."

The pup released tentacle man and plopped him down on the sand.

The bandit gripped his torn neck, trying to staunch the flow of blood. The pup panted, tongue lolling from her blood-stained mouth.

"Thadd." Annora knelt beside him.

He glanced over and saw that the guy she'd been

fighting was sprawled on his back on the sand, not moving, his neck at an odd angle.

"I'm all right." Thadd rubbed his neck, then swiped his arm across his stinging eyes.

Annora touched his skin and looked at the bruising. She turned, her hot glare zeroing in on Tentacle.

The guy froze.

He should've bled out by now, but Thadd saw the man's wounds were slowly knitting together. His species clearly had enhanced healing abilities.

"Don't move," she warned.

Thadd suddenly felt warm wetness on his cheek. The pup had shifted closer and was licking his face.

*Gorr*. He fended the wolf-dog off. It looked at him with adoration.

Annora made a sound. "I see you've made a friend." The pup eyed Annora suspiciously. The animal could obviously smell the wolf on her. Then it tried to climb into Thadd's lap.

He pushed it off, but did give the pup a quick scratch behind the ears.

"Why don't we ask our new friend some questions?" Thadd suggested silkily.

Tentacle man tensed even more.

Annora formed her claws, holding them up.

The bandit stared, mesmerized. Then he swallowed.

"How long have you been here?" she asked.

Tentacle shrugged. "Years. Got caught stealing off a Sarkan ship." He turned his head and spat blood onto the sand.

"Are there any installations close by?" Thadd asked. "Bases? Ships?"

Tentacle's lips moved, then he laughed. "This is *Krone*. The Sarkans don't let *anything* off, and they don't put anything useful here. You get dropped on Krone, you die here."

Annora leaned forward and pressed her claws to the man's midsection.

He sucked in a breath.

"Answer the question." Her voice was low and deadly.

Auroras, she was gorgeous.

"There are no gorr-cursed bases. There's nothing. The Sarkans leave nothing. They don't even land their ships. They just drop prisoners out onto the sand." The man sucked in a breath.

Annora met Thadd's gaze. He nodded.

She straightened and withdrew her claws. "Go."

Tentacle sat frozen for a beat, then he scrambled up. He jogged away at a hobbling run.

The wolf-dog pup growled.

Thadd rose, rubbing his sore neck. The pup moved over and sat on his boot.

Annora looked down and her lips twitched. "You guys are cute."

He grunted. The wolf-dog looked up at him, a goofy look on its face. With a sigh, he patted the animal. It made a disturbing sound, but seemed happy.

"We need a plan, Thadd." She pressed a hand to the back of her neck. "Naberius is up there, turning that genite into some weapon to wipe out the Talnians. I am not letting him get away with it."

Thadd's jaw clenched. "We'll keep searching. We'll find a way off this moon, or wait until Rhain and Brodin arrive."

He pulled her into his arms, and she pressed her face to his shoulder.

The pup growled at her.

She laughed. "Sorry, dog. He was mine first."

Thadd stilled. She met his gaze, then quickly looked away.

Gorr, he liked being claimed by her.

"Let's find some water, then get out of the sun for a bit," she said. "Then we'll keep looking around."

## CHAPTER FOURTEEN

Annora crouched and scooped up a handful of sand. She watched the sand particles stream through her fingers.

In the dying light of the day, she scanned the desolate, sandy landscape.

Nothing.

They'd searched all day for anything to help them get off Krone.

Nothing.

Her belly was filled with knots. She felt like every second was an hour. Plenty of time for Naberius to move a step closer to hurting so many people.

There would be Talnian girls, just like Nayla in the line of fire—innocents, someone's daughter or sister, someone with a life ahead of them.

She blew out a breath.

She didn't hear him, but she sensed him. A warm hand pressed to her shoulder. In such a short time, she'd become so attuned to this man.

"It's only been one day so far," Thadd said. "Don't lose hope."

"I won't." Annora rose and turned to face him. "But I'm allowed to be frustrated as hell."

"You are." He touched her cheek. "I feel the same way."

"But you're doing your stoic Zhalton warrior thing, and not letting it show."

He gave her a faint smile. "Want me to shout? Break some rocks?"

She smiled back. "Maybe."

He tugged on her braid and pulled her in for a kiss.

From nearby came a soft growl.

"Really?" Annora rolled her eyes and glared at the pup. It glared back at her, jealousy in every line of its body. "Is that creature going to get jealous every time I kiss you?"

"She has good taste."

Annora elbowed him.

"Come on. We should head back to the grotto before nightfall." He glanced around. "I'm pretty sure we don't want to see what creeps out around here at night."

They started back toward the rocky cliffs. Thadd's new friend jogged at his feet.

As they reached the area strewn with large boulders, the wolf-dog paused and growled.

"What now?" Annora muttered.

"I'm not sensing anything," Thadd said.

A small lizard creature scuttled over a rock. It was covered in overlapping brown scales.

The pup went still, its body quivering, its gaze locked on the little reptile. Then she pounced.

The lizard dodged the canine and took off at a blinding speed. The pup gave chase.

"Looks like you've been ditched for a reptile, Naveri."

He reached out and pinched her butt.

She hid her smile. Despite the circumstances, he was less stiff, more playful. It was nice to see him that way.

There was a sudden crack of noise.

They looked up and saw churning clouds gathering over the cliff.

*Gorr.* "It's not a sandstorm," she said.

Thadd eyed the boiling, black clouds. There was another flare of lightning and another crack of thunder. "It looks like a regular rainstorm."

He took her hand, but they hadn't made it back to the cliff before the rain hit.

The deluge hammered down. Instantly, her hair was soaked. The only good thing was that the water wasn't cold.

Thadd tugged her under an overhang of rock. "It's too dangerous to climb the cliff in this."

Another brilliant spear of lightning hit. The sandy ground turned mushy from the water.

Thadd pulled her closer to his body. As usual, heat pumped off him.

She saw movement on the ground and her lips parted. "Thadd, look at that."

Green shoots pushed up through the sand. Little plants appeared all over as the rain continued to fall. The plants bloomed with white flowers, growing like they were on fast-forward. They looked like tiny dancers. The flowers formed a pretty carpet all around, and gave off a faint glow.

"I guess there is something about this place that's beautiful," she said.

"Well, just don't touch them. They'll probably poison you or eat you or something."

She laughed, then went up on her toes and kissed him.

His arm snaked around her, one big palm cupping her ass. He took control of the kiss.

"I hate that we're stuck here." His mouth traveled down her neck. "But I'm glad you're here with me, Annora."

Her heart swelled. She tilted her head to give him better access. "I'm glad you're with me too."

His mouth took hers again, and a flare of heat shot through her. His kiss was deep, drugging. She knew the taste of him so well now.

His hands skimmed up her body.

"I need you," she whispered against his lips.

She did. Not the frenetic rush of lust, underscored with anger and dislike that had started this. Now she felt something deeper, hotter, more important.

His hands found the fastening of her suit. He opened it and pushed it down as the rain continued to beat down around them, locking them in a private cocoon.

His lips and hands moved down her chest. One calloused palm cupped her breast as his warm mouth caught her nipple. She sighed his name, her hands in his hair.

She managed to fumble on the fastening of his suit. It parted and she shoved the top down.

"I love your chest," she panted, stroking the hard muscle and warm skin.

"I'm quite partial to yours too." He lifted her off her feet.

By claws and fangs, she loved his strength.

He pressed her against the warm stone as she wrapped her legs around his waist. Their gazes locked, neither one of them closing their eyes or looking away.

His breath mingled with hers. Their lips touched. They continued to stare at each other as they kissed.

Annora felt something deep inside her shift and change. She felt laid bare, like he could see straight through to her wolf, her soul. Flutters of panic winged through her.

"Annora." He took her mouth again.

The panic subsided, because she realized she could see into his soul as well.

This big Zhalton warrior had opened himself for her, letting her see what he kept hidden. His strength, his vulnerabilities.

Him.

The man she realized she was falling for.

The head of his cock nudged her. He held her gaze as he slowly slid inside her.

Consumed. She felt taken, cherished, absorbed.

With every thrust of his powerful body, she felt a part of her unravel, then thread together with him.

His hand slipped between them, and found her

swollen clit. He held her tight, stroking as he pinned her against the rock wall, thrusting deep.

"Thadd—" She couldn't form any other words. Strands of hot pleasure wrapped around her, shot through with so much emotion.

He kept thrusting, and stroking.

Her orgasm ripped free. She clamped her arms and legs on him, crying out, trying to muffle the sound by biting his shoulder.

"Mine," he groaned. "My gorgeous, strong wolf."

On the next thrust, he stayed buried deep, groaning through his own release.

Then, there was just the drum of the rain and the sound of their harsh breathing.

He kissed the tip of her nose.

It was sweet, and very un-Thadd like. She smiled. She loved it.

Her heart did a hard *rap-rap* in her chest.

*Love.* Oh, claws.

She shoved it down deep. Soon, if they managed to stay alive, she'd have to deal with the fact that she loved all of him.

He set her down. They cleaned up and she put her suit back on.

Annora held her cupped hands together and held them out under the rain. She drank some water. Then she wrang out her hair and re-braided it.

She didn't bother to pretend that she wasn't watching Thadd's body as he pulled his suit up.

He caught her and his lips quirked. "After this, I want you in a bed. A big, soft one."

They were clearly on the same wavelength. "I like your thinking, Naveri."

He cupped her cheek.

Suddenly, the rain slowed. There was a sound, and the wolf-dog pup reappeared, soaked, with blood around her mouth.

She glowered at Annora, before rubbing against Thadd's leg.

He stroked the pup's head, while Annora rolled her eyes. The canine shifted, then shook herself, sending water splattering over Annora's suit.

"You menace." Annora shook her head.

Suddenly, there was a loud rush of sound in the sky.

Thadd and Annora stiffened and spun.

Through the dying rain, they saw a ship fly overhead. Its lights lit up the growing night darkness.

Its *landing* lights.

She met Thadd's gaze, then they both watched as the ship set down on a small sandy plain in the distance.

THADD LEAPED OVER A BOULDER, running silently, Annora beside him.

He grabbed her arm and they slowed. They were almost at the ship.

They crept stealthily the rest of the distance, and ducked down behind a tumble of rocks.

The pup sat beside him, body quivering. The ship had seen better days. Its hull was made of a dull gray metal and scratched. It had a solid, rectangular body, with sturdy wings that had folded downward when it landed. It had a small tower at the back, probably housing the cockpit. It also had several gun turrets on top.

A ring of landing lights illuminated the sand around it. As they watched, a ramp opened at the front.

"Merc ship," Annora murmured.

"It's a Sarkan design, but it's old."

"It's junk."

Two heavily armed men in battered armor appeared on the ramp. They both cradled huge laser weapons in their arms.

"This moon is a dump," one grumbled.

"But it has good hunting." The other mercenary sounded younger. "I tell you, Nax, if you want any credibility as a merc, you have to sneak onto Krone and kill something here." The younger guy jerked his gun. "There are *all* kinds of gorred-up beasts here, not to mention half-crazed prisoners."

Nax grunted. "We already have a good gig, Talock. Once we deliver our current cargo, we'll score a big payday."

"Yeah, but here, we get to kill stuff, and no one cares." The young merc thumped the chest controls on his armor. A single weapons sight flicked open from the neck of his armor and sat over his right eye. He sounded pretty eager to get to the killing. "Let's kill some ugly monsters!"

"These two sound like winners," Annora muttered.

"I want the ship, not them." Thadd's eyes gleamed in the low light. "We'll wait for them to get far enough away, then we hijack the ship."

She eyed the ship. "It's a rusty heap of junk."

"If it gets us off this moon, I don't care."

"All right, but I hope you can fly it."

"We'll work it out."

Not exactly a ringing endorsement.

The mercs stomped off. It wasn't long before they disappeared into the darkness, their voices drifting back until they faded.

Thadd and Annora waited a little longer. The pup snuffled quietly.

In the distance, laser fire and raucous laughter carried on the wind.

"Idiots. They'll attract every beast or prisoner within earshot," Annora said.

"Let's try to be gone before that happens," he said, rising. "Let's move."

They darted out of cover. The ground was still wet from the storm, sucking at their boots. They crossed the open ground toward the ship.

Suddenly, Thadd felt a tingle on the back of his neck.

He paused, scanning around.

"What?" Annora asked.

"Do you sense anything?"

She stiffened. "No."

The pup growled.

Thadd saw lots of rocks, crouched like beasts. There was a trickle of energy, but nothing that—

One of the rocks burst to life. The beast unfolded, and its energy punched into Thadd. It must've been hibernating.

The creature made a horrible sucking sound and stalked toward them.

Annora cursed.

This had to be a failed Zhylaw experiment. The stench of old blood and rot wafted over them.

The creature moved on four powerful legs. It had pink-gray skin stretched tight over streamlined muscles. Two tentacle-like protuberances rose up over its shoulders from its back.

It had a head, but no mouth. There was just a gaping maw. Then three tongues shot out, waving madly.

"Oh, gorr," Annora muttered. "Disgusting."

Patches of the beast's skin were raw, oozing fluid. Thadd realized it had eyes. About a dozen of them scattered erratically over its head. He'd never seen anything so wrong or ugly.

It made another sucking noise and ambled closer.

"Keep it busy," she said.

*Sure.* Thadd pulled his bone blade.

He stepped forward, grabbing the creature's attention. Its tongues wobbled madly, like they were picking up sensation.

The two tentacles on its back rose up, and the tops of them unfurled to uncover sharp, bone-like spikes.

*Great.*

Thadd ran, and the beast lunged. He spun and rammed the bone blade into the creature's side.

It made a horrible choking sound, but the bone barely penetrated the gristly muscle.

He whipped around, and one of the tentacles stabbed at him. Cursing, Thadd threw himself to the ground.

The appendage and its bone spike stabbed into the sand beside him.

There was a flash of movement and the pup leaped into the fight. It latched onto the tentacle, its fangs sinking deep. The pup growled, gnawing on the beast. Black blood seeped down the tentacle.

Thadd leaped up. The second tentacle aimed for the pup, ready to stab it.

*No.* He jumped and swung the bone blade as hard as he could. It sliced into the tentacle. He pushed hard, felt the squelch of skin and flesh. The severed top of the tentacle fell to the ground with a plop.

The creature made more wild sucking noises and shied back. The other tentacle lifted into the air, and the pup held on to the injured one. The tentacles waved wildly, trying to knock the tenacious dog free.

The beast's head whipped around, and its three tongues snapped at Thadd like snakes.

That's when he heard shouting. He glanced over and saw the mercs sprinting back toward them.

*Gorr.*

Suddenly, a huge shape sailed through the air and landed on the back of the Zhylaw beast.

The large wolf's claws slashed at the creature's flesh. With a lethal swipe, the wolf cut through a tentacle and the pup jumped free.

The beast made a loud, wet noise and bucked.

Annora leaped off gracefully, turned, and attacked.

Laser fire hit the sand nearby. Thadd spun. The mercs were nearly on them.

He raised his hand. Power coalesced, energy-rich and strong. He tossed his arm to the side and both mercs flew to the left, one falling on top of the other.

He turned back. Annora had savaged the beast. It was done, lying on its side and flailing weakly. She swiped at it again, ripping its side open.

Annora's wolf padded over to him. She was big, powerful, with dense black fur and gold eyes.

"Beautiful." He stroked her fur—it was softer than it looked.

"Hey! Get away from our ship."

The mercs were both back on their feet. They had their weapons aimed at Thadd.

He felt Annora's muscles tense, and then she pounced.

The huge Damari wolf slammed into the younger merc. The older one swiveled his weapon around then fired on her.

Thadd's gut clenched, and he held up his hand.

The merc froze. The man tried to move, but he was held in place by Thadd's energy. The man gritted his teeth, straining.

Thadd strode closer. The man's weapon crumpled with the crunch of metal. Next, Thadd squeezed. The man's armor pressed inward, like a crumpling can.

The older merc's eyes went wide. "No. *No.*" The words were choked. He clawed at his armor.

Thadd didn't kill the man. He let the man drop to the sand, trapped in his crumpled armor.

Annora was changing. He looked away until she strode out of the darkness, sleek and naked.

"Let's go." She snatched up her discarded suit, confident with her nakedness.

Together, they ran up the ramp of the ship.

The pup followed.

"You should stay here." Thadd stroked the wolf-dog's leathery back. "This is your home. Go on."

Big, brown eyes watched him, then the pup bounded after Annora into the ship.

Thadd shrugged. He cast one more glance at Krone. *Time to get out of here.*

## CHAPTER FIFTEEN

The ship shuddered as they left the planet's atmosphere.

Beside her, Thadd's face was like rock, his hands clamped on the console. Behind them, something crashed.

Annora looked back. A rusted panel had popped off the wall. The inside of the ship was just as junky as the battered outside. Not to mention it smelled.

The ship jerked, and she was tossed forward against her harness, the straps biting into her skin.

"Everything all right?" she asked.

He adjusted something on the console, and the jerking decreased. "I have no idea. I hope so."

"That's reassuring, Naveri."

"Do you want to fly?"

Flying was not in Annora's skill set.

Moments later, they broke free of the atmosphere, and the shuddering thankfully stopped.

Thadd touched something and they swung around, heading away from the dark bulk of Sarkan.

Annora glanced down at Krone. *Good riddance.*

A wild squawk echoed through the ship from the cargo hold, followed by the sound of thumping.

*Gorr.* What the hell did the mercs have aboard? She unclipped. "I'll go and check it out."

"Be careful."

She took a second to touch his broad shoulder and squeezed.

Annora headed back through the filthy living area. A built-in table was covered in dirty plates and trash.

Her nose wrinkled. More screeching came from the cargo area. She paused at the weapons locker, and found it woefully understocked. She took a knife and a small blaster, and slipped them both onto her belt.

It took two slaps on the door sensor for the cargo doors to open. Gorr, this ship might be more dangerous to them than Krone.

The door opened and the horrible stench of animals in close quarters hit her.

Annora breathed through her nose, cursing her acute senses. She took in the cages retrofitted into the cargo area. In several, she saw creatures—alien reptiles, something small and fluffy clinging to the bars, some things she couldn't identify.

A bird creature, almost as big as she was, fixed her with a beady stare and flapped its giant wings before squawking angrily.

She checked the system that watered and fed them.

Everything looked like it was working correctly. Then she swiveled and headed back to the cockpit.

"The mercs have been hunting," she said.

"I'm not surprised." He touched the controls. "I'm not sorry we left them on Krone." He touched the controls again. "Damar? Is anyone picking this up? Come in, Damar?"

Annora dropped into her seat. "You can't make contact?"

"No." Frustration was ripe in his voice. "I don't think the signal's getting through."

"It's not surprising. The Sarkans jam and control all signals around their planet."

Thadd's hands moved over the console. A projection popped up in front of them. A dour-looking Sarkan with a thin face and disapproving stare looked back.

"Recorded message," Thadd said.

"Nax, please bring the alien specimens to Abiosis station as soon as possible to fulfill your contract."

Thadd and Annora straightened.

"The mercs were en route to Abiosis," she said.

"Naberius wants those specimens you promised yesterday," the Sarkan continued. "He's putting the finishing touches on an extremely important project that he's planning to deploy soon. If you want your payday, don't be late."

Annora's hands clamped on the console. "It *has* to be the genite weapon. He's perfecting some way to deploy it on Taln."

A muscle ticked in Thadd's jaw. "Yes." He tapped on the console, then swiped. The ship changed trajectory.

A second later, Annora saw the distinctive shape of the space station in the center of the viewscreen.

"We aren't heading to Damar?" she asked.

He looked at her. "We haven't finished our mission."

She smiled. "No, we haven't."

"Go find some merc armor. We're going in as mercenaries. We're going to find Naberius and his weapon, and blow them both to tiny pieces."

She leaned over and kissed him.

When Thadd groaned, cupping the back of her head, she rose. If she kissed him any longer, she'd wind up in his lap, and they didn't have time. Unfortunately.

It took a while, but she found the merc's sorry stash of armor. It wasn't in great condition, but there was enough here to help Thadd and her look the part.

She pulled the smallest set of armor plates on. It was battered, scratched, and there were a few laser scorch marks. She bundled her hair up in a bun, then pulled on some spacer goggles. She pushed them up on top of her head.

She needed to look less First Claw, and more wild, lawless mercenary.

She set out some armor for Thadd, then she headed back to the cockpit.

He eyed her outfit. "You look...interesting."

She snorted. "I set some stuff out for you. I'm hoping you can manage to look less—" She waved a hand.

"Hygienic?"

She smiled. "Less well-trained Captain of the Guard."

"I'll see what I can do." He pushed out of the pilot's seat. "Don't let us crash."

Out of the viewscreen, the Abiosis was getting larger. She watched a ship fly out of it.

She wasn't sure if they'd survive this. She dragged in a deep breath. But she was glad Thadd was with her.

Whatever happened, she would do her duty, and she wouldn't fail her people.

She'd also fight hard for the man who now meant so much to her.

She fished her chain out from under her shirt and thumbed the charm on the end from Nayla. She loved her family, her friends, her fellow cleavers, Brodin. And she'd now added Thadd to that list.

A part of her wanted to tell him, but she had no idea how he'd react. They were about to con their way into enemy territory. It wasn't the time to bare her soul.

She hoped they'd have time later.

The thump of heavy footsteps made her look over her shoulder. She stilled.

Thadd always held himself straight and tall. It was clear he was a man with dedication, control, and training.

But the man who strode toward her now had a touch of swagger. His mismatched merc armor was strapped over his spacesuit. His forearms were bare, and he had a metal ammo ring clamped around one bicep, filled with tiny explosives.

He looked like a dangerous rogue.

"You look..."

He scowled. "Ridiculous."

"Hot," she countered.

His eyebrows rose, and he shot her a smile. "Save that thought for later."

If they had a later. The thought sat, unsaid, between them.

He grabbed her hand and knelt in front of her. "It's you and me, Annora. We're going to stop Naberius and save Taln. Together." His lips quirked. "This Damari I know has taught me a thing or two about teamwork."

She cupped his cheeks. "Really?"

"Really."

"Together," she said.

The ship's console chimed.

Thadd sat back in his seat. Abiosis station filled the viewscreen.

"Approaching ship, identify," a voice rasped on the comm.

"This is the mercenary ship, *Hammer*. We're here to make a delivery."

There was a pause, and Annora's pulse jumped. What if they weren't fooled?

"*Hammer*, you're cleared for landing. Dock Three. Follow the docking bot in."

A small, disc-shaped bot covered in blue lights flew up in front of them.

"Here we go," Thadd said.

"Here we go."

---

THADD STOOD beside Annora as the ramp of the ship lowered.

A harried-looking Sarkan strode up, barely looking at them. He was staring at the comp pad in his hand.

"Right, we'll transfer the specimens out," the man said.

"They're in the cargo hold," Thadd said.

"Right. Right." The man swiped his comp pad.

Thadd hated the idea of any creature being handed over to Zhylaw scientists, but if they succeeded here today, they might be able to save some of the people and creatures aboard the space station.

The look in Annora's eyes said she wasn't all that thrilled about handing the creatures over either.

"You can head to the guest level," the Sarkan dock worker said. "There's food in the mess and relax facilities. If you need supplies for your ship—" he eyed the Hammer with faint distaste "—talk to logistics people on Level Alpha Sixteen."

"Thanks." Thadd tipped his chin up.

Thadd and Annora strode off, crossing the docking bay.

"That was easy," she murmured.

Other ships were parked nearby, disgorging cargo. Busy workers moved all around the cargo level.

A wild, enraged roar filled the space.

Thadd and Annora stepped to the side as workers pushed a heavily fortified crate past them.

The creature inside roared again, the sound of claws scratching on metal making Thadd wince.

He and Annora made it out of the docking area, and headed up to the guest level. As they neared the guest mess, he heard the racket of conversation and noise in the kitchen area. At a glance, he saw a motley assortment of mercenaries inside.

Without slowing, he and Annora bypassed the doors, looked around, then slipped into the main corridor.

"Let's get up to the dome and find Naberius' lab," he said.

She nodded. "And if we run into guards or security bots?"

"Then we tell them that we've been authorized to deliver special cargo to Naberius himself."

"What cargo?"

"The top-secret kind that we can't talk about." His face was serious, and it was impossible to tell that he was lying.

They hit the escalator. They passed some Sarkan and Zhylaw, but no one even blinked at them.

Then, they reached the level below the dome.

"This way," he said.

Screams echoed off the walls and they both froze. Thadd looked down at the shiny floor, and heaved out a breath.

Annora touched his back.

"I'm okay," he said. "Let's keep going. This is the only way to help the people here and save Taln." They needed to kill Naberius and disable the space station.

They reached the labs. There were floor-to-ceiling glass windows that looked in. Three tanks, with creatures floating inside, dominated the space. Several Zhylaw scientists watched the central tank, and a second later, the occupant of the tank started thrashing around in the fluid.

Thadd's jaw locked. When Annora nudged him, he dragged his gaze away.

The door into the dome opened and they were assaulted by the rich, lush scents of the vegetation.

He realized that they were coming in from the other side of the dome to last time. Here, the trees and vegetation were a little different, a little more sparse. He saw a long, sinuous reptile draped from the branch of the tree.

Agonized screams echoed through the dome, startling birds into taking flight.

Then he heard voices.

Thadd grabbed Annora's arm and they ducked into the dense bushes. Two Sarkan workers strode past.

"Naberius tests my patience," one grumbled.

"Let's just be glad we're out of his lab for the day." The female worker shuddered. "Some of the things he does..."

The workers disappeared out of the dome.

Thadd glanced in the direction the pair had come from. "It looks like it's this way."

He and Annora moved fast. A door appeared ahead, and they stopped in front of it.

His heart hammered, and he fought back the memories.

Then he looked at Annora. She just watched him—no judgment or pity. Just her usual quiet strength.

*Gorr.* He was in love with her.

It was a hell of a time to realize that.

She nodded at him, then pressed the door sensor.

The door whispered open without a sound. Inside, the lab was dark.

They stepped in, scanning around. There were rows of benches on one side, and darkened cells on the other. A faint mist hung in the air. In the back, screens were filled with data, glowing brightly in the low light.

There was no sign of the Zhylaw warlord.

Thadd and Annora moved across the lab.

The creature strapped to the nearest table had its gut flayed open.

Thadd tasted bile.

Annora grabbed his hand and squeezed.

Suddenly, the creature moved weakly.

*Gorring hell.* It was still *alive.*

Thadd grabbed the knife he'd taken from the weapon's locker on the ship, but Annora moved faster. There was a flash of claws, and she ended the creature's suffering.

"Come on." Her mouth was a flat line.

They moved through the lab. There were more dead creatures, and signs of torture.

Naberius had to be stopped. There was no sign of him, or the genite.

They neared the cages. A wild, blob-shaped beast attacked the bars, hissing and spitting. It didn't appear to have a head or limbs of any kind.

"Thadd?"

Annora was at a workbench. He strode over to join her.

And that's when he saw what she was looking at. There were bright blue chips of genite scattered on the surface of the bench. *What the gorr had Naberius created?*

And where was it?

"We have to find out what he's done." She reached over and swiped a nearby screen.

Words flashed up in the Sarkan language.

She cursed. "Security is too tight. I can't get in."

*Gorr.* He pressed his hands to his hips. They couldn't search the entire space station for the Zhylaw. It was enormous and they'd be caught.

Failure bit at him, along with that gorr-cursed sense of helplessness that he hated.

In the cage, the blob creature went wild again, slamming against the bars. In the cell beside it, Thadd saw a small shape shift in the shadows.

He took a step closer, frowning. Whatever was in there, it was watching them.

"Okay, the space station must have security feeds," Annora said. "My suggestion is we break-in, and find Naberius on the feeds."

"Or we stakeout the ships leaving the space station?" Thadd countered. "Spot him when he's leaving with the weapon."

Annora released a breath, touching a shard of the mineral. "I just wish we knew what the gorring weapon was."

"I saw it," a quiet female voice said.

They both whipped around to face the dark cell.

It was a female in there. She'd moved closer to the bars, but her face was still in shadow.

From her silhouette, she was small.

"You saw it?" Annora asked.

"I watched him make it. Using the blue jewels." The

woman paused and swallowed audibly. "He...integrated the crystals with some small slug creatures."

"What?" Annora breathed.

"I believe they're going to put them in the river systems of some planet. The creatures will procreate and spread the poison through the water."

"Gorr!" Thadd wanted to hit something.

"I'm sorry," the woman whispered.

"You have nothing to be sorry about," Annora said.

"But I do." Her voice sounded broken. "He... He uses my blood. It helps him make his creations."

The woman stepped forward, into the light.

She was tiny, with pale skin and dark, choppily cut hair. She wore loose gray trousers and a sleeveless shirt.

She wasn't emaciated or starved. She looked clean, and it was clear that Naberius kept her well fed and well looked after physically.

Then Thadd saw the scars covering the woman's arms. They weren't huge, but in the right light they showed. They were score marks from a knife.

Annora gasped, staring at the woman with the huge green eyes in a pale face.

Thadd frowned. Annora stepped closer, a strange look on her face. She looked fascinated by the woman.

"Annora?" he said.

She continued to stare at the woman. "You're from Earth."

The woman in the cage stared, her eyes widening and her face got impossibly paler. "Yes. I am."

# CHAPTER SIXTEEN

Annora used her claws to rip open the lock.

The woman stepped out.

She looked well-fed but pale. She was tiny, but she had curvy hips and full lips. She looked like a doll that Nayla had played with as a baby.

But there was defiance in this woman's pale green eyes. Her spirit wasn't broken.

"What's your name?" Annora asked.

"Evie. Evie Mason."

"How long have you been here, Evie?" Thadd asked.

She shrugged a shoulder. "I'm not entirely certain. My best guess, about two years."

*Two years.* Horror and sympathy filled Annora. She saw the scars up the woman's arms.

Two years of being locked up.

Two years as Naberius' plaything.

"How did you get here?"

"I'm guessing we're a long way from Earth?" Evie said. "My home planet."

"Earth is on the other side of the galaxy," Annora told her quietly.

The woman squeezed her eyes closed. "I was the logistics manager for an exploration ship. We were doing survey work for a space station in my star system, orbiting a gas giant called Jupiter."

Annora frowned. She'd talked with Poppy about life on Earth. "The Resilience Station?" That couldn't be right. That station was currently being constructed.

Evie's brow creased. "No. Fortuna space station. It's a state-of-the-art science station." She cast a contemptuous glance around the lab. "Nothing like this place. We were out of range of Fortuna, running surveys, when our ship was attacked by aliens." She wrapped her arms around her middle. "I don't remember much. I woke up in a cell, and I never saw any others from my ship. I was told they were all killed." She swallowed. "I was sold to Naberius."

*Gorr.* Annora lowered her voice. "Evie, Fortuna station was destroyed in an alien attack over a year ago."

Evie's face wobbled. "*No.* How do you know this?"

Annora held out a hand, like Poppy had showed her. "Let's start at the beginning. I'm Annora Rahl, of the planet Damar."

"The Damari are shapeshifters. Naberius has mentioned Damar." Evie took Annora's hand and shook it. Tears welled in her eyes. "God, I haven't willingly touched someone in so long."

"You're safe now. We're getting you out of here. This is Captain Thadd Naveri of Zhalto."

He nodded at her.

"And you know about Earth," Evie said.

ANNA HACKETT

Annora smiled. "I have a friend from Earth. The mate of my emperor, and the future Empress of Damar. Her name is Poppy Ellison."

Evie's lips parted. "How is that possible?"

"And the future Queen of Zhalto is also from Earth," Thadd added. "Mallory West."

"How? I haven't seen another human in all this time."

"Mal and Poppy were testing an experimental starship," Thadd told her. "They careened through a wormhole and crashed on Zhalto."

"Mal is a pilot and Poppy is a scientist." Annora smiled. "They'll be so happy to meet you."

Evie pressed her hands to her cheeks. "I've been—" her voice hitched "—alone for so long."

"There are other humans close by as well," Annora said.

"What?" Evie breathed.

"On the planet Carthago, in the neighboring system. When Fortuna was attacked, several survivors were abducted by alien slavers. They were sold on Carthago, but have been rescued and taken in by locals. They've made a life there."

A tear fell down Evie's cheek. "I... That's incredible."

"Look, Evie." Annora touched the woman's arm and felt a weird tingle.

The woman stiffened for a second, then relaxed.

"Sorry." Annora lifted her hand.

"It's okay. I just haven't been touched for any other reason than torture for a very long time."

Annora battled back another flood of sympathy. "I know there's a lot to take in. We aren't leaving you here.

204

We're going to get you out, but we have to stop Naberius first. And the weapon he's made with the genite crystals. He's planning to attack our allies, the Talnians. Genite is lethal to them."

"He's made a small army of those genite slugs," the woman said.

"Do you know where he is?"

Evie straightened. "Yes."

Annora's pulse spiked. "Where?"

"He took the slugs to the water lab. To test them before deployment."

The water lab. Annora met Thadd's gaze. They had to stop the warlord.

"Do you know the way?" Thadd asked.

Evie nodded, horror dancing in her eyes. "I do."

They followed the small woman out of Naberius' lab. Annora saw that Evie was limping a little, and wondered just how tough she'd been to survive for so long.

They took a left, then headed out of the dome.

"The water lab is directly below the dome. Run-off from when they water the plants trickles into the water lab." She stumbled and Thadd reached for her.

She stepped back and held up a hand.

"I'm okay. I've got it. Come on."

They moved into the corridor. Evie stopped at a door. When she opened it, Annora saw a set of stairs leading down.

They jogged downward, and at the bottom, they moved back into another corridor.

"The entrance to the water lab is at the end of this hall," Evie said.

They rounded a corner and almost slammed into a Zhylaw scientist. The male had an implant covering half his skull. Shock hit his face. "Who are—?"

Annora moved. She slammed the man against the wall, then punched him.

The Zhylaw were not a physically strong species, relying on their brains instead of their bodies. The man collapsed with a gurgle.

"That was badass," Evie breathed.

"I'll teach you some moves when we get back to Damar."

A smile bloomed on the woman's mouth. "I'll take you up on that." Then she jerked her head. "This way."

They followed her down the hall and stopped at a shiny silver door. She squared her shoulders.

"Ready?"

Thadd nodded. "We're ready."

Evie touched the sensor and the door opened. Annora fought back a gasp.

The water lab was *huge*. It was filled with several connected pools. Some were built higher, dripping down into others. Steam wafted off several, and lots of them were filled with fluid of different colors. Clear pipes also ran from some pools, along the walls and ceiling.

"It's huge," Annora murmured.

"I don't see Naberius," Thadd grumbled.

"Come on." Evie stepped onto a path. "He's here. Don't touch the water. It's filled with bad things."

They followed the woman. The path twisted through the pools. Annora saw a shadow move in the depths of one pool. A reptilian creature rose up, showing the spikes along its back, before disappearing back into the water.

She suppressed a grimace.

Then she heard voices.

"Push him in. *Now*." Naberius' imperious voice.

"No!" A man's pleading cry. "Let me go."

Annora, Thadd and Evie hurried forward.

Annora spotted Naberius first. He was standing at the edge of a pool, an excited gleam on his scarred face.

A guard came into view, holding a struggling Talnian. *Oh, gorr*. It was *Hagen*.

"You promised me wealth! A new life! So I could save my child."

Naberius cocked his head. "You will have a new life, in the beyond." A smug smile. "So I didn't lie to you."

"No!" Hagen fought.

Annora looked at the pool. It appeared placid and clear.

Then she saw the fat slugs, glowing genite blue, sitting on the base of the pool.

She ran forward.

Hagen's terrified gaze locked with hers.

"I'm sorry," the pilot choked out.

The Sarkan guard shoved the man, and Hagen hit the pool with a splash.

---

A STRING of curses ran through Thadd's head.

Hagen thrashed in the pool. At first, he seemed fine,

then the pilot began screaming. He clawed at his face, struggling to stay afloat. His skin was...melting.

*Gorr.*

Thadd hated that the man had betrayed them, but he hadn't wanted this.

"Get them!" Naberius yelled, glaring at Thadd and Annora

Thadd whipped back and lifted his laser rifle.

The Zhylaw's gaze fell on Evie. "Get the small woman! She's mine."

Beside them, Evie stiffened. "I'm not going back." A fierce whisper. "I'm not going back to that cell."

"Come on." Annora fired her blaster. The three of them ran sideways around a pool.

Thadd kept firing. Energy swelled inside him.

"We need to kill the slugs," he yelled.

"And not let Naberius sneak out like the cowardly snake he is," Annora added.

Their gazes met.

"It ends here," Thadd said. "Today."

She nodded. "It does."

So beautiful, strong, and fierce. "Let's do this, First Claw."

"I'm with you, Captain."

He laid down laser fire.

Naberius' guards started firing back, shielding Naberius.

Annora grabbed Evie, and the women ducked down behind the edge of a pool.

In the closest pool, Thadd saw green, bubbling sludge

growing. He had no idea what it could do, but he was certain it wouldn't be good.

Naberius and the guards were out of sight now. He heard laser fire right beside him and jerked.

Annora was firing into the slug pool.

He darted toward her. Someone fired at him, and he felt a sting on his arm and gritted his teeth. He fired back and ducked down.

"You okay?" Annora asked, casting a worried glance at his arm.

"It's fine."

Despite the circumstances, he saw her roll her eyes.

Evie bit her lip, staring at the pool.

"I tried firing on the slugs," Annora said. "But the pool is deeper than it looks, and the laser isn't reaching them."

They saw Hagen, floating face down, his blood seeping into the water around him.

"*Gorr*." Naberius wanted to do that to all Talnians—man, woman, and child.

His jaw hardened. The Zhylaw had to be stopped.

"Naberius will try to escape," Evie said. "He's a coward. And for all his enhancements, he's more delicate than he likes to admit." A small, feral smile. "I cut him once with a shard of metal. He bleeds."

"We'll deal with the slugs, then Naberius." Thadd stared at the glowing creatures in the water. They seemed so harmless.

He held up his hand.

Energy came to him, strong and powerful.

A slug rose up out of the water. "Do it."

Annora aimed her weapon and fired. The slug burst, flesh dropping to the water with a splash.

Evie grimaced.

Two more slugs rose up. Annora shot them as well.

They repeated the process, over and over. He used his senses to feel along the base of the pool for the creatures' dull life signs.

With a whirr of laser, the next genite slug exploded.

"No!" Naberius' shout furious. "Stop them."

Laser fire winged past them. They ducked. The slug that Thadd had just lifted fell back into the water with a splash.

"We're pinned down," Annora clipped. "There are only three more slugs."

Evie's face hardened. "I can help. I can lead them away—"

"No." Annora shook her head. "We're sticking together."

Evie bit her full lit, and looked conflicted. Then she straightened her shoulders. "I can still help." She looked at Thadd. "Can I...touch your arm?"

It seemed he'd healed a little, because that question didn't give him a violent, knee-jerk reaction. It helped to know she'd been through something similar to him, so much worse than everything he'd suffered.

He nodded. "Okay." He wasn't sure what she was planning.

Evie pressed her small hand to his forearm.

He felt nothing, but then a second later, it felt like her palm was heating up. He frowned.

"It won't hurt," she said. "I promise. I'll distract Naberius' guards while you kill the final slugs."

The small woman's green eyes changed, glowing the same blue as Thadd's.

He sucked in a sharp breath. He sensed Annora tense.

Evie rose, energy crackling around her.

Then she threw up both hands. A Sarkan guard rose into the air, struggling. Evie thrust her hand to the side. The man's body flew through the air and hit a pool of water with a giant splash.

Someone fired, but she deflected the bolt.

"Don't kill her!" Naberius cried. "She's too valuable."

Thadd stared at Evie. He still felt his own energy humming in his veins.

But she'd somehow absorbed his powers.

Annora shook her head once, like coming out of a daze. "Thadd, the slugs."

He focused back on the pool, still aware of Evie causing havoc behind them. He focused and lifted the slugs up out of the water.

Annora fired. Once. Twice.

The last slug hung in the air, glowing blue.

Another blast of her weapon and it disintegrated.

"Done." She smiled. "The slugs are all destroyed."

"Now Naberius." If they didn't kill him, the Zhylaw would just create more slugs. Cause more harm.

"Let's split up," she said. "I'll come from behind."

He grabbed her for a quick kiss. "Be careful, *thistla*." Other words and emotions welled inside him. He wanted to tell her that he was falling in love with her, but now wasn't the time.

She smiled. "I'm always careful." Then she darted away around the pool.

Evie used her powers, tossing a discarded weapon at a guard. The man ducked.

Thadd scanned around, but didn't see Naberius.

"Where's the scum?" he said.

"He pulled back." All of a sudden, Evie wavered on her feet.

Thadd grabbed her arm. "You okay?"

"Your abilities are pretty potent. I feel a bit lightheaded."

"You'll have to explain all this later."

An unreadable look crossed her face. "I'm not sure I can. What Naberius did to me... I'm not the same."

The gorr-cursed Zhylaw. Hurting so many people.

"The Zhylaw warlord Krastin tortured me recently. I'm not the same either. But that doesn't mean we give up, or don't deserve to live. We have to adjust, adapt."

She blinked at him.

"It's going to be okay, Evie. Now, let's get some justice."

The woman's eyes, still blue like his, gleamed.

"Fuck yeah," she said.

They both rose and they threw their hands out.

Several guards tumbled, weapons hitting the floor. They shouted, scrambling to recover their guns. Sensing a life form in the pool to his left, Thadd levitated it up. The creature came up snapping its sharp teeth, its tail thrashing. He tossed it at the guards. The men dived for cover.

"Come on." Thadd and Evie raced down the path between the pools. The ones ahead gleamed pink and green.

Then he spotted Naberius trying to make a run for it.

"It's over, Naberius," Thadd yelled.

The Zhylaw stopped and looked back. "No, it's never over. With my genius and innovation, I plan to live forever. And my patron wants that too."

Those words were like a fist to the gut. Zavir wanted to live forever?

*Gorr.* The thought was horrifying.

Naberius had sprinted out of sight.

*No, you don't.*

Thadd and Evie rounded a raised pool. That's when he saw Naberius facing off with Annora. She stood tall, unafraid, her claws out.

Annora advanced on the Zhylaw.

Naberius whipped up a small, unfamiliar weapon.

Evie stiffened. "Watch out!" She leaped, trying to tackle Naberius.

But the man flung out a hand and hit her. She fell hard. Thadd saw her head bounce off the edge of the pool before she slumped to the ground, still and motionless.

The weapon shot out a bubble of energy. The blue bubble expanded and hit Annora.

*No.* Heart lodged in his throat, Thadd ran.

Naberius shot them a look, then raced deeper into the lab. Escaping.

# CHAPTER SEVENTEEN

Annora growled. The bubble of energy around her glowed. She touched it and pushed.

There was no give.

It sizzled a little under her fingers, but it didn't hurt. She pressed both palms to the surface and shoved.

Nothing. It felt like a solid wall.

"Annora!" Thadd appeared on the other side. He laid an unconscious Evie down on the ground.

Annora's heart thumped. The poor woman had been through so much. "What's wrong with her? Is she hurt?"

"She bumped her head trying to stop Naberius shooting at you."

"These women from Earth don't lack courage, do they? Will she be okay?"

"She has a bump on the head, but her pulse is steady. I think she'll wake up soon." Thadd threw his weight against the energy wall.

It sizzled, but was unchanged. With a growl, he rammed his shoulder into it.

"Thadd, I'm not sure brute strength will do it."

"It's energy."

And energy was his thing. But this was something cooked up by Naberius.

Thadd pressed his palms to the bubble and closed his eyes.

She felt the flare of energy, and watched his face getting grimmer and harder.

"Thadd—?"

"I'm getting you out," he roared.

She sucked in a breath. She knew his overprotective instincts were in overdrive.

He pulled back, a snarl on his lips. He shoved his hands against the bubble and pushed again.

How could she have ever thought that this man was selfish and hungry to be a hero.

He *was* a hero. A warrior to the core. Built to protect.

A bellow escaped from him as he kept pushing, pouring his power against the energy bubble.

She saw the strain on his face grow, the pain in his eyes.

Then his nose started to bleed.

*Enough.* "Thadd!" Her heart clenched. "Stop."

"No. I'm getting you out."

"*Stop.* You're killing yourself. Please, stop."

His rugged face twisted, but reluctantly, he let his hands drop. His blue eyes were burning as he stared at her.

"You need to go and stop Naberius," she said.

He shook his head violently. "No. I'm not leaving you behind."

"I need you to trust me. I will get out of this...thing. You need to keep Evie safe and stop Naberius. If he keeps breathing, then Taln is not safe."

Thadd looked away, a muscle in his jaw ticking.

"Thadd. I trust you to go and stop him. I'll catch up."

He looked back at her. "I know. I've never met anyone as smart or strong as you... But I still don't like gorring leaving you behind."

"I know."

She touched her fingers to the energy barrier. He lifted his hand and touched hers from the other side.

She could almost imagine that she felt his skin.

"Go." Her voice was thick. "Don't get hurt."

He managed the tiny nod, and then his hand dropped away. He knelt, then tossed Evie's slack body over his shoulder.

"Stay alive, Annora, and hurry. I'll be waiting for you."

She nodded.

"The energy is somehow coded to you. I don't know what it means, but it...it feels a little like you."

She frowned and nodded. *What the hell did that mean?*

"See you soon, Annora."

"You sure will, Naveri."

"That's not what you call me."

Memories and emotions cascaded through her. "Thadd." She cleared her throat. "Go."

He turned and walked away with powerful strides. Evie's weight didn't seem to bother him.

Annora's hand clenched. She watched until his big body disappeared.

*Right.* She needed a way out.

She tested the bubble shell all around—top, bottom, sides. There was no apparent sign of weakness. *Coded to her?* It must be a part of the weapon. That's how it kept a particular person trapped inside and everybody else out.

She tried a few kicks and punches. Nothing.

She growled. Naberius was scum. Very annoying, smart scum.

Pressing her hands to her hips, she wished she could pace, but the bubble wasn't big enough.

Wait.

Coded for her. But Annora wasn't just a woman. Hmm, she wondered if it would work.

She had nothing to lose.

She quickly slipped off the armor and spacesuit. She willed the change. Her muscles stretched and shifted, and her wolf took over.

Annora's senses sharpened. She hit the ground on all fours and lifted her head.

She was inundated by scents, sounds, and sights.

The energy bubble shimmered before her. Then her thermal vision kicked in.

The energy wall wasn't as solid as it seemed. It was riddled with cracks that looked gold. Where it was more solid, it gleamed blue.

She padded up to it and pressed. It bulged outward.

*Yes.*

She kept pushing. The crack widened. Almost there. She lifted her paw and rammed her claws into the crack.

Then she threw all the weight of her wolf into it.

Ever so slowly, the crack widened.

*A bit more. A bit more.*

The energy bubble burst, and Annora spilled out.

She threw her head back and let out a howl of triumph.

Quickly, she changed back. She had to sit for a second, shaking and sweaty. She'd changed back and forth too much recently. But her wolf form wasn't suited to a space station.

After yanking her suit back on, she grabbed her laser blaster and took off at a jog.

She needed to find Thadd.

She needed to take down Naberius.

She leaped over a small pool and raced out the door. Out in the corridor, she heard the distant echo of laser fire. She saw workers running along the corridor, panicked.

"What's happening?" she called out.

"Fighting," one said. "Stay clear. There are intruders aboard."

Annora picked up speed. She sprinted down an escalator. There was more laser fire.

Her belly clenched. Thadd would be fine. It would take more than a bunch of Sarkans to take him down.

She heard running footsteps, and darted into a doorway.

A group of guards jogged past. She waited, then followed them.

*Hold on, my Captain. I'm coming.*

As she neared the docking bays, there was pandemonium. She needed to get in there.

Suddenly, someone grabbed her arm.

She spun, lifting her claws.

*Evie.*

The woman looked pale and had a bruise on her temple.

She tugged Annora into an alcove.

"Where's Thadd?" Annora clipped out. "Are you all right?"

The woman swallowed, and pushed her messy mop of dark hair out of her eyes. "They took him."

"What?" *No.* Dread pooled in Annora's belly. "What happened?"

"He risked himself to save me. He barely knows me. They captured him." Anger and sorrow churned in the woman's green eyes. "They took him to Naberius' lab."

Annora felt the floor heave. *No.*

---

WITH A GROAN, Thadd opened his eyes.

His head throbbed, his mouth was dry. *What had happened?*

A stunner to the head would do that.

*Gorr.* The guards had gotten him when he'd shoved a still-dazed Evie out of the way. He shifted his arms, but couldn't move. Panic, slick and oily and horrible, filled him.

He was strapped to a bench.

Tied down.

He swallowed, staring at the huge leather straps.

The same ones Krastin had used on him on Zhalto.

Krastin was dead. Thadd fought to remember that. He felt like there was a rock in his chest. He battled not to hyperventilate and looked around.

They were back in Naberius' lab. He saw the cages, Evie's still open. The blob creature hit the bars, wild and savage.

Trapped. Like Thadd.

*No.* He closed his eyes and thought of Annora. The image of her helped him, and he calmed a little.

Annora would get free.

She'd come to him.

The gorgeous wolf had taught him teamwork. That he could depend on others, and they were stronger together.

He drew strength from that.

*She'd come.*

"Ahh, you're awake."

Naberius stepped into view. He looked a little shaky, his hair was disheveled, his scars standing out on the burned side of his face.

He was holding an injector filled with a green fluid. Thadd stiffened, bile in his mouth. His pulse raced like a ship at top speed.

But Naberius pressed the injector to his own neck.

A second later, the man shuddered, his face going lax. He seemed to relax.

"Ahhh, that's better." He tossed the injector aside. "Now, you meddlesome Zhalton. I plan to make you hurt." Anger flared on his face. "You destroyed my weapon. The genite karggites."

Thadd figured that was the proper name for the slugs.

"I'll start again, but you've set me back." Naberius toyed with some tools on a nearby tray. "Zavir is not forgiving of delays."

"Yeah, I'm so sorry." Thadd let sarcasm fill his voice.

"You also took something valuable of mine." Naberius' voice turned low, menacing.

Thadd glared at the Zhylaw. "You mean Evie? She's a person. She can't and won't ever belong to you. You can't own people, you gorr-ridden scum."

"She's mine!" Spittle flew, and Naberius' mechanical eye moved wildly. "Her blood. It's special. It's made it so easy to force my tech adaption on my experiments. She's special."

*Adaption?* Thadd frowned. Mal had picked up Zhalton abilities. Poppy had been infected with the Damari virus, but her body had adapted in her own unique way. Was something about the blood of the Earth women special?

Naberius had kept Evie locked up, draining her life blood, for his own terrible purposes.

"Evie is free now. You'll never get your blood-stained hands on her again. My overlord and his brothers won't allow it."

"Your overlord and his brothers are on borrowed time. Zavir never stops, never gives up. He'll bring them to heel. He stepped softly so far with those imbeciles

Krastin and Candela." An ugly smile. Naberius lifted a thin knife. "I will not be so nice."

The scientist moved closer and Thadd's chest locked. Old memories pushed up.

*Think of Annora. Think of being in her arms.*

But he couldn't relax this time. His muscles strained against the leather bindings.

"I'll make an example out of you, Captain. A warning to anyone stupid enough to oppose me or Zavir."

Naberius pressed the blade to Thadd's chest.

Thadd hissed, and absorbed the stinging. He gritted his teeth as the scientist cut him.

He would not yield. He would not show this monster his fear.

Naberius took his time, opening up more cuts.

Thadd stared at the ceiling of the lab. A groan slipped through his clenched teeth.

But he wouldn't scream.

The pain increased to a terrible burn. Naberius hummed, pulling out more gadgets.

"I will make you hurt. Your screams will echo through the station. Your trapped Damari will hear you."

"You're...a Gorr," Thadd pushed out.

Naberius sneered and jabbed the blade into Thadd's chest.

Thadd groaned.

"I'm a genius. I'm the best scientist on Sarkan, of the Zhylaw, in the entire system."

"You're just filth. And we all know you're the one on borrowed time. I can smell your rot." Thadd stared at the

Zhylaw. "Your body is failing you, isn't it? Soon you'll just be a rotted corpse. A forgotten, ugly footnote."

"I'll *never* die. And if I did, I'll leave a legacy behind."

Thadd managed a scoffing noise. "Zavir will replace you in a flash."

"I can't be replaced!" Naberius yelled.

He threw the bloody knife in his hand. It sailed across the lab and hit an empty bench with a clatter.

The blob creature went wild, slamming into the cell bars.

"I will kill you painfully. Then I'll kill your Damari whore. I'll put the Earth woman back in a cell. And then I'll kill so many Talnians, its conqueror will cave. Zavir will shower me in adoration."

Thadd choked out a laugh. "Never... Going to happen."

Naberius lifted a small, boxy device and jammed it against Thadd's chest. Electricity hit, skating over his skin. His body shuddered, and his teeth clamped together.

The pain was worse than anything. He bit his lip. He wouldn't scream. He smelled his flesh burning.

*Annora would come.*

The energy cut off. He slumped and felt tingly all over. Energy filled him.

Naberius turned the device on again.

Pain drenched Thadd, but this time, he was ready. He pulled the energy into him.

"Hurts, doesn't it? I'll leave nothing but a burned husk by the time I'm done with you."

Thadd tasted blood in his mouth, and his vision grayed.

He had to stay conscious.

Naberius lifted the device again. "Next, I'm going to—"

Thadd lifted a finger. Power poured from him in a rush.

It hit the Zhylaw and lifted him off his feet. Naberius flew back and slammed into a bench. He screamed.

"Who's...screaming now?" Thadd pushed out.

Naberius shoved himself up. His face was a pale, pale blue, and some of his hair was singed.

"I'm going to *kill* you, Zhalton." He snatched up an implement with two sharp prongs on the end and staggered forward. He loomed over Thadd, raising the tool. "I'll start with your eyes."

Thadd stayed impassive, but inside he was anything but.

He had a piercing realization that he loved Annora Rahl. He wasn't falling. He was already there.

She pushed him, challenged him, supported him. She was strong, but tender. Fierce, but loving.

He wished they'd had more time.

He braced himself as Naberius lowered the tool.

A wolf leaped over him, aiming for the Zhylaw.

Annora crashed into Naberius with a snarl.

## CHAPTER EIGHTEEN

S he knew Thadd was hurt, and back in the nightmare that he couldn't escape.

Annora's anger was hot and wild.

Naberius rose and she growled.

The Zhylaw froze, staring at her. His lips trembled. "You'll never get off this station alive."

Annora didn't give a flying fuck. Another saying she'd learned from Mal.

She walked toward the scientist. Her priority was ending this monster.

For Nayla.

For the Damar.

For the Talnians.

For Thadd.

No more suffering. Naberius was a symbol of all the hurt and pain that Zavir had rained down on all of them.

She swiped out with her claws.

Claw marks opened up on Naberius' chest. He cried

out and stumbled back against the bench. Items fell, crashing to the floor.

He stared at the wounds, his face pale and panic in his eyes.

He eagerly cut open others, but he couldn't cope now the tables were turned.

He barely bled. A very dark, black blood oozed at the edges of the wounds. His breathing was fast and shallow.

There was a flash of movement in the corner of her eye.

Annora noted Evie yanking the straps off Thadd.

She'd seen the blood. She had no idea how badly he was injured. *Please be okay.*

Naberius grabbed things off the bench blindly—implements, devices. He threw them at her. Some sailed past Annora. A few hit her fur, and fell to the floor harmlessly.

She growled, lifting her paws and advanced.

Naberius shakily circled the bench, trying to get away from her. The creature on it, chained down, screamed.

The scientist kept stumbling.

"You're an animal," he screamed. "I'll kill you."

If she could roll her eyes in wolf form, she would. Only one person was dying here. Her wolf was enraged, out for blood. This man had hurt her mate.

*Mate.*

The word echoed with certainty inside her.

She felt a throb in her chest, and felt the mating link. The connection to her mate.

*Oh, Gorr.* There would be complications for sure, but she loved Thadd Naveri.

Her mate.

She leaped, swiping with her claws.

Naberius cried out and ducked under the bench, crawling on hands and knees.

She leaped onto it.

He looked up at her, fear in his eyes.

Just like all his victims had felt.

Annora leaped, taking the Zhylaw flat to the floor. She sank her fangs into his neck.

He screamed. She tasted horrid, nasty blood, and lifted her head, shaking it.

The man flailed beneath her, but she kept him pinned.

"You fucking asshole monster." Evie stepped into view, Thadd behind her.

The top of Thadd's suit was slashed up, his bare chest peeking through. He was covered in angry slice marks. Blood flowed down his skin.

Annora growled. Her mate was hurt and she didn't like it.

Thadd gripped the back of her neck, and stroked her fur. "I'm all right. Thanks to my fierce wolf."

Evie glared at Naberius. "You took me prisoner. You *stole* me. You treated me like a specimen. I am a *woman*. A woman from Earth. You destroyed my life." She snatched up a thin surgical knife off the tray. "Now I'll destroy yours."

She dropped to her knees and stabbed.

Naberius screamed.

As Evie attacked the scientist, Annora kept him pinned for the woman.

She looked up at Thadd. She expected to see the same need for vengeance, but he was watching dispassionately, and surprisingly calm.

He stroked her back again. "I'm really okay."

She leaned her head against him.

"You are a gorgeous wolf."

As Naberius' screams slowed, Thadd had clearly reached a limit.

He picked up a large knife off a bench.

"Time to dance with the auroras, Naberius, and be measured for your crimes."

Thadd knelt on one knee and slit Naberius' throat.

Annora wondered if Thadd saw Krastin's face as he did it.

The Zhylaw scientist went still, and lay sprawled on the floor, a stunned expression on his scarred face.

Evie sat back, staring at the blood on her hands.

"I thought it would make me feel better," she whispered. "I've watched him hurt so many people, creatures, beings."

Thadd was watching the woman steadily. "It didn't help?"

A flash of a smile. "Oh, it did, but it's not enough." She leaped to her feet, the knife slipping from her hands. She strode towards the cells.

All the creatures inside were agitated. The blob creature was wilder than normal.

Evie swiped furiously at a comp panel.

"What are you doing?" Thadd asked.

"Righting some wrongs."

The cell doors started to open.

*Oh, Gorr.* Annora tensed.

Creatures flew out, mindless and out of control.

"Go!" Evie yelled. "I've unlocked and decoded all escape pods on the station. All the shuttle bay doors are unlocked. Get off this place. Go home."

The cell door for the blob opened.

"Evie." Thadd stepped in front of the small woman. Annora flanked him.

"It's too dangerous," he said.

"No. He won't hurt us."

The creature slithered out, body oozing as it moved.

It paused, seemed to look at Evie.

"He just wants to get back to his family," she said.

Then the blob shifted, racing across the lab frighteningly fast, and shot out the door.

Evie went back to work on the comp screen. "I've opened all the cells." A smile flirted around her lips. "In every lab on the station."

"Auroras above," Thadd murmured. "How do you know how to do this?"

"I worked in logistics. I had to be adaptable on our survey ship. I knew every system from the kitchen to the cargo bay. This space station isn't that different." She tapped some more. "And next..." More taps. The lights in the lab turned red and alarms blared. "I've voided all experiments and tanks into space." She swiped.

Suddenly, there was faint movement under their feet. Annora realized the space station was starting to list to one side.

"I've also cut off power to the station stabilizers." Evie's smile was sharp. "Abiosis is going down. I suggest we get off it before it hits the Sarkan atmosphere."

"Evie—" Thadd began.

"It ends here. Naberius is gone, but there are others like him. There are so many people trapped here, who have been here for so long. In so much pain." She straightened. "I've given as many as I can a chance. Some won't make it—" she pulled in a shuddering breath "— and some are changed. Some... They won't want to make it off. I understand that."

"You're coming with us," he barked. "You have others from Earth who will do everything to help you."

Evie's green eyes locked on him, then moved to Annora.

Annora moved to the woman, brushing against her.

Evie grabbed a handful of Annora's fur and let out a ragged shaky breath. "Okay. I'll come with you."

"Good," Thadd said. "Now let's find a ship and get off this hellhole space station."

---

THADD HOBBLED DOWN THE CORRIDOR, trying not to lean too much of his weight on Annora.

She'd changed back from her wolf form. He could tell she was still a little shaky. She'd changed too many times in a short period of time.

But her jaw was set in its usual stubborn line.

"Naveri, lean on me. I'm Damari, I can handle it." She scowled at him. "Or I'll carry you."

*Not happening.* He leaned a little more on her.

The pain in his chest had coalesced into a throbbing ache. The cuts weren't bad, but he'd lost a lot of blood and felt weak. Annora looked at his chest and her face darkened.

"I want to kill Naberius again," she muttered.

"He's dead already, *thistla.*" And Thadd felt a savage sense of satisfaction about it.

"Come on," Evie called back.

The other woman was ahead of them, blaster in hand.

The space station was tilting, and the floor under their feet felt like a ramp. They were heading to the docking bay to find a ship.

The emergency lights washed everything in red. The alarms were echoing down the corridors.

They headed out into a central atrium. Panicked people were running and screaming. There were Sarkans, Zhylaw, workers, prisoners, mercenaries. Everyone was trying to get off.

All of a sudden, several large cats raced into the crowd. They'd clearly escaped from a lab. People leaped aside. One cat snarled and took a swipe at a Sarkan woman.

The cats continued their mad dash. One neared Thadd's group. It lifted its head, its eyes filled with sharp intelligence.

It sniffed, and then its gaze settled on Annora. It bared its fangs.

Annora growled, and the cat stared for a beat, then took off with the others.

"The Annora Rahl glare and growl," Thadd said. "No one can withstand it."

She pinched his side. "You can. You always could."

He met her gaze. "I kind of like it." He lifted his fingers and stroked her neck. "Thanks for freeing me."

"You had to be going crazy in there."

"It wasn't fun, but I knew you'd come."

There was deep emotion on her face, strong and intense. "I'll always come."

But suddenly, the floor tilted sharply. Screams echoed and people started to slide. A few smacked into walls, or collided with others.

Evie cursed and caught herself.

Thadd and Annora clenched on to each other, catching their balance.

"We need to move," Evie said. "Or there'll be no ships left."

They hustled out of the atrium and down a long corridor. They weren't far away from the docking bays now.

Three Sarkan guards and a female Zhylaw scientist barreled out of a doorway.

The guards lifted their weapons, but Evie fired first.

The woman laid down blast after blast of laser fire. Guards fell with a cry. The others grabbed their injured and scrambled back into the room.

"We're almost there," Evie said. "Hurry."

They reached the first docking bay, just as the ship left. A gust of hot air blasted through the space.

There was laser fire. Several mercenaries were shooting each other, trying to board the final ship.

"The next bay," Annora yelled.

They ran. The next bay was empty. There were no ships left.

Thadd's gut curdled. They might be stuck here.

They kept moving. They picked up speed, Thadd pushing his body to move faster.

They burst through the doors to the next docking bay.

Three mercenaries and a Sarkan worker were heading toward the same battered, hijacked ship that Thadd and Annora had arrived on.

Annora let Thadd go and he planted his feet.

"That's our ship!" Annora yelled.

"Go and gorr yourself," a tall, scaled female mercenary yelled.

Evie fired.

Annora's claws shot out. She flew at the female merc. The others continued running for the ship, dodging Evie's fire.

They couldn't let them get to it first.

Thadd raised his hand. He pulled energy to him, thick and fast. Then he fired off a pulse.

It hit the Sarkan man, and he tumbled and fell. The other two mercs tripped over him.

Thadd moved forward, cursing his injuries.

The two mercs leaped up, swiveling their rifles around.

Thadd made both the guns fly out of the mercs' hands, then twist around each other like he was tying rope.

"Gorr," one muttered.

Then Evie's blast hit him in the chest. He spun and fell.

The final merc turned and sprinted for the ramp of the ship.

*No.* Thadd moved forward, but he knew he'd never catch him in time.

Suddenly, a shape darted out of the ship and down the ramp.

With a vicious howl, Pup launched herself at the merc. She clamped her fangs on the man's legs, growling.

"Gorr!" The man tried to shake the pup off.

Thadd strode the rest of the way and punched the merc. The man collapsed like a wet blanket.

"Good girl." He patted Pup. Her tongue flopped around, her body shaking with happiness.

He turned, just in time to see Annora leap into the air, and land a brutal kick to the female merc's chest.

The woman flew back and hit some crates with a loud crash.

*Magnificent.* When he looked at her, he saw pride, desire...and love.

Annora sprinted to the ship. Evie limped up the ramp.

"Let's go." Annora gripped Thadd's cheeks, pulled his head down, and smacked a kiss to his lips. "I've had more than enough Sarkans and Zhylaw for today."

They hurried inside the ship.

"Evie, strap into one of those side passenger seats," Thadd ordered. "And take care of Pup."

The Earth woman nodded.

"Pup?" Annora asked.

"I found a name for her."

"You're such a man."

"Which I believe you're pretty happy about."

Thadd and Annora settled in the cockpit.

"No time for preflight checks." He touched the take-off sequence on the console. "We need to go now."

"Punch it, Chewie," Evie said from behind.

Thadd frowned. "What?"

"Um, just an Earth saying. Go."

Thadd looked at Annora, and then the ship shot forward.

They blasted out of the docking bay. Ships were flying everywhere, and escape pods littered the space around the station.

Thadd adjusted course. They stared at the tilting space station.

"Good riddance," Annora muttered.

Evie unclipped and came forward. There was a dark look in her eyes as she stared at Abiosis. At the station that had been her prison.

It started to hit the atmosphere of Sarkan, flames flaring up over its bulk.

"Let's put some distance between us and Sarkan," Thadd said.

The ship picked up speed.

Somewhere behind them, something rattled, broke loose and fell with a crash.

They all ignored it.

Annora smiled. "I can't wait to get back to Damar." She lowered her voice. "And my very comfy bed."

His gut clenched tight.

"Did I mention it's big?" she added.

"No."

Her smile widened.

Then, an insistent chime started.

"What's wrong?" Evie cried.

Thadd tapped the controls. "Hang on. It's the proximity scanner." A projection appeared on the screen.

It showed a huge ship incoming from behind.

It was bullet shaped, and made of a dark metal. It had three prongs at the front, a long body, then it flared open at the back. It was easy to see the purple glow of the engines.

It was a Sarkan interceptor.

And it was hunting them.

# CHAPTER NINETEEN

Annora stared at the Sarkan ship. It was built to dominate and intimidate.

The Sarkans excelled with ship design. Warship design. She knew it would be packed with weapons.

A sense of helplessness threatened.

They'd gotten away. They'd stopped Naberius and the genite slugs. They'd rescued Evie.

This wasn't fair.

But life never was. She'd already learned that in her role as First Claw, in defense of her planet, and seeing her sister and her friends snatched by a warlord.

And knowing what had happened to Thadd only underscored it.

All you could do was pick yourself up and deal with it.

And lean on your loved ones when you needed help.

"Our rust bucket is no match for that interceptor." Thadd's tone was dark.

She looked at him. "I love you."

His eyes flashed. "Annora—"

"If someone had told me just weeks ago that I'd be so in love with you, that I knew that I could depend on you, I wouldn't have believed them. In fact, I would've thought they'd lost their minds."

"You've made your point," he said dryly, but he was smiling. "I love you too."

She pulled in a deep breath, wonderful emotion blooming inside her. She realized that some of what she was feeling was his emotion, thanks to their mating bond.

"If anyone had told me that weeks ago," Thadd said. "Well, I might've confessed to a raging attraction that I tried to hide. And a deep admiration and respect. But I wouldn't have believed love. I believe now."

She leaned over and kissed him.

"We're fighters," she said.

"We are," he agreed.

"No surrender. We run, and if that isn't an option, we fight."

He inclined his head. "I like that plan."

The viewscreen flashed.

The face that appeared made every single muscle in Annora's body lock.

King Zavir of Sarkan didn't look like a megalomaniac killer. In fact, Brodin's father looked regal, handsome. He had a touch of gray at his temples, but the rest of his hair was a rich black. He looked like the kind of man who inspired trust.

It made him infinitely more dangerous.

"First Claw Rahl. Captain Naveri. A pleasure to see you both."

Neither Thadd nor Annora responded. She sensed Evie listening carefully behind them.

"Please power down your engines. I'm inviting you aboard my ship so we can talk."

*Right.* Annora leaned forward. "We respectfully decline."

There was a quick, almost missed tic at the corner of his mouth. "I insist." Some of Zavir's lazy charm disappeared. "You destroyed a very valuable asset."

She looked at Thadd. "I'm not sure if he means Abiosis, Naberius, or the genite slugs."

That muscle ticked again. "I grow weary of my sons all defying me. Now they send their agents into the heart of *my* territory." Zavir smacked his fist on the table in front of him. "I won't stand for it."

"You were planning genocide on Taln, you cracked gorr-scum," Annora bit out. "Neither Brodin nor Rhain would allow that. And Graylan will protect his planet. I don't think you understand just what you're stirring in the conqueror."

No, Graylan hid it well, but he was strong, intense, and filled with a deadly power. He showed everyone a charming face, but her wolf sensed it.

Zavir's face twisted. "You destroyed Naberius, and my science station. I will make you pay."

Annora smacked the console and cut the call. "That's enough of that."

"He sounds like a nice fellow." Evie's voice was light, but Annora heard the fear the woman was trying to hide. Her hands were clenched in the pup's furry collar.

The woman had probably guessed that Naberius' boss had to be worse.

"Buckle in," Thadd said.

A new alarm sounded.

"The interceptor has primed weapons," Annora said.

*Gorr. Gorr. Gorr.*

"Get those turrets activated," Thadd said.

That she could do. She accessed the weapons controls. Firing this merc ship's turrets would be like tossing twigs at the Sarkan ship. She shrugged. She preferred to be fighting back any way she could, rather than simply sitting there thinking of surrendering.

The turrets lifted up and fired.

"Hang on." Thadd threw their ship in a bone rattling, gut-churning dive.

The merc ship shuddered and rattled. Something broke loose in the back, fell, rolling across the floor before it crashed into something. There wouldn't be anything left by the time they got out of there.

When he leveled them out, the interceptor was practically on top of them.

Annora's heart did a giant leap into her mouth. "Thadd!" He'd flown them *toward* the Sarkan ship.

"That interceptor is less maneuverable than us. We'll drive them crazy, then make a run for it."

"Sneaky. I didn't know you had it in you."

He flew them in a wild, erratic pattern. The turrets scored some hits, and there were times the interceptor fire missed them, hitting itself.

Oh, she'd give anything to see Zavir's face right now.

Thadd wheeled them around. "Here we go."

Annora pressed her palm over his. "I'll follow you anywhere, Captain."

Even into the beyond, if that's where they ended up today.

They shot free of the bulk of the Interceptor. Thadd pushed the merc bucket for every drop of speed.

The Sarkans weren't fooled for long. She watched on the scanner as the giant ship raced after them.

It was gaining.

Annora released a breath. They weren't going to make it. She threaded her fingers with Thadd's.

"When they take our ship aboard—"

"We blow our engines," he said.

She smiled. They were on the same wavelength.

They looked back at Evie. Her face was solemn, but she smiled. "Hell yeah! Make those assholes regret everything."

Thadd managed to coax more speed from the ship. They were hurtling through space.

Then suddenly, a giant, black ship blinked into existence right in front of them.

Annora gasped. With a curse, Thadd changed their course so they didn't collide. Still, they got pretty close. They missed the black ship by a whisper.

Annora's heart lifted, emotions crashing into her. "It's a Talnian ship."

Another ship appeared. It was a stream-lined silver design, trimmed in red.

Thadd smiled. "That's the Zhalton flagship, the *Genesis*."

Another smaller ship, made of brown metal, appeared. It was Damari.

The ships opened fire on the interceptor.

Laser fire lit up the space around them.

And then came the most beautiful sight of all. The interceptor turned tail and fled.

"Oh my God!" Evie yelled and clapped. Pup leaped into her lap, licking her face.

The viewscreen flashed.

The three kings appeared on screen: Brodin, Rhain, Graylan.

"Are you all right?" Brodin growled.

For once, Annora didn't respond to her Emperor. She unclipped her belt, dizzy with relief. Then she cupped Thadd's face and kissed him, uncaring that they had an audience.

He kissed her back.

"Well," Graylan sounded amused.

"I think they're just fine," Rhain drawled.

---

THADD WOKE and stretched in the large, comfortable bed.

It wasn't his, but he couldn't complain.

He opened his eyes, his gaze going straight to the huge floor-to-ceiling glass window across from him. The curtains were open, giving an unobstructed view of the city of Gearma on Taln.

A huge, pointed mountain peak dominated, capped

with snow. The city's buildings dotted the mountainsides all the way down to the steep valley below.

Thadd and Annora had been picked up and taken to Taln. He ran his hand over his chest. The Zhalton medicas from the *Genesis* had healed him.

There were no scars. No pain. It was almost like it had never happened. Like everything had been a dream.

Like he'd never touched Annora, fallen for her, given himself to her.

But the sheet smelled like her. And he sensed her energy close by—strong and true.

It filled him, as did the energy of Taln.

He finally accepted that his abilities were not the same as they had been before.

They were better, easier for him to use.

That wasn't a bad thing. In fact, they would help him do his job even better.

After the medicas had seen him, and he and Annora had showered, they'd fallen into bed, and dropped into a deep sleep, tangled up with each other.

The bed beside him was empty right now, though. He smoothed a hand over the covers.

Then he saw Annora step inside from the balcony.

She wore a long, shimmery, silver nightgown. It coasted over her curves. Her dark hair was loose and looked soft.

She saw him and smiled.

He'd sell his soul for her to smile at him like that all the time.

Though, he loved all of her looks. Her First Claw glare; her fierce, fight frown.

"You shouldn't be out there without a coat," he grumbled. "It's cold."

"Don't worry, I'm Damari. We don't feel the cold as much." She paused. "How are you feeling?"

"Good. Very good."

She walked toward him, and his gaze traveled over her. So beautiful. His body took notice.

"We survived." She sat on the edge of the bed.

"We did. Together. I'd never have made it without you."

Her dark gaze traced over his chest, and he knew that she still saw the wounds, though he was now fully healed.

"I'm physically fine, Annora. No scratch or cut left."

Her gaze flicked to his. "I wish Naberius had never touched you."

"I knew you'd come. And he's dead. It's hard to worry too much about a dead guy. I guess I finally realized that no one lives their lives without picking up a few scars. That isn't something to be ashamed of. It's a sign of honor. A sign you stood up and fought."

"A sign you survived," she said.

He nodded. Speaking of survivors... "How's Evie?"

Annora sighed. "Okay. She's been checked over, and she's healthy. But she's not settled or relaxed. I think she has a long, hard road ahead of her to heal—mentally and physically."

He understood that. More than most. "She just needs time. And people who care."

"She has that. And Mal and Poppy are spending time with her."

"Evie will be fine. Eventually. Come here, Annora."

Color filled her cheeks. "We finally have a comfy bed." She rose, then slipped the straps of her gown off her shoulders.

The silky fabric slithered down her body. She was naked underneath.

He drank her in eagerly. *His.* She was his, just as he was hers.

They'd never been enemies, but definitely rivals.

Now she was his love.

She crawled across the bed toward him. His cock tented the sheet.

She straddled him and stroked his chest. "I love you, Thadd."

He cupped her jaw. "I love you too, Annora. I've avoided entanglements my entire life, despite my mother's insistent matchmaking attempts."

"You poor thing. Someone foisting beautiful women off on you."

"It was easy to avoid things getting serious. I'd never felt like this. Never thought it possible to feel so much for someone." He ran his thumb over her lips. "Now, I can't imagine my life without you. I want you at my side. Ready to take on any challenge."

"Thadd." Her face turned soft. She pressed her lips to his.

They'd started in fire and anger, but now that had changed to something stronger and deeper.

"My Captain." Her gaze met his. "My mate."

He sucked in a breath. "I...felt the tug, but I wasn't sure."

"It means you're mine." She sank her teeth into his bottom lip. "And I'm yours. I'm not letting you go now."

"Good." He yanked her down, plunging his tongue into her mouth. "I need you."

"I need you too." She undulated against him.

Desire ignited and turned into an inferno. His hands stroked up her body, found her nipples.

"*Yes*." She shimmied against him.

"You're beautiful," he said.

Her dark eyes opened, drenched in love. "So are you. Hot, hard, impossible to resist."

He surged up and caught her mouth again. He slid his hand down her toned belly, between her legs, and found her clit. He rubbed it and she moaned for him. Then she was shoving the sheet aside.

Her hand closed around his throbbing cock.

He cursed.

He nipped her neck. She rubbed against him and pressed her face to his skin. He realized she was drawing in his scent.

He kept circling her clit, and thrust two fingers inside her. She rode his hand, her breathing turning to harsh, needy pants.

"*Thadd*."

"Come for me, *thistla*."

Her body clenched on his fingers. She arched, crying out.

He loved watching the pleasure overtake her.

"Again," he growled.

She made a sound, but a second later, she orgasmed again.

She was boneless and lax when he gripped her hips and lined up his cock.

As he lowered her, he thrust up, sinking inside her. Her eyes shot open.

Annora moaned. He gave her body a second to adjust to the stretch. She slowly took over, riding him hard, her inner muscles squeezing him, as her hands pressed to his chest.

The pleasure grew, the world shrank. Her hips moved faster.

"Annora." A gritty growl.

"I love you. I love this. I love my mate inside me."

Thadd roared. He reared up and flipped her onto her hands and knees. He gripped her hips, then thrust back inside.

"My mate. My Annora." He thrust harder, plunging deep inside her tight warmth.

When she came again, he did too.

Pouring himself inside her, he heard her cry out his name.

In that moment, Thadd had everything he'd never known he wanted.

## CHAPTER TWENTY

Annora smoothed her hands down her dress. It was a traditional Damari dress with a modern twist. It was one of her mother's designs.

The flexible leather bodice fit her like a glove, and was a lovely pale gold. It was strapless, except for one strip of leather that crossed over one shoulder. From the bodice, white fabric fell to the floor, and a high split showed one leg.

Beaten metal circled her waist, and matching metal circled one bicep. She also wore a fine circlet of gold that rested on her hair. She'd left her hair loose, but pulled back from her face.

"The ceremony is ridiculous," she complained. "Completely unnecessary."

"It's not for you," Thadd said from the bathroom that adjoined their room. "It's to let the Talnians celebrate that Zavir didn't succeed. For them to rejoice that there wasn't mass genocide on their planet."

Annora made a harrumphing sound. She didn't love

being the center of attention. She preferred doing her job off to the side. Protecting without fanfare.

They'd been on Taln for two days. They'd spent that time relaxing, recovering, and recharging. For her and Thadd, that translated to a lot of wandering the streets of Gearma. And sex. Lots of fabulous sex.

Even now, she was tingly all over from when he pinned her to the wall earlier and made her scream. She shivered.

But now, they had to attend a ceremony in their honor.

Rhain and Brodin had updated them. The Sarkans had managed to stop Abiosis from falling to the planet surface or burning up. It was back in orbit, but heavily damaged. She smiled. There would be no experiments or tortures on that station anytime soon.

Her smile faded. The only dark spot was Evie.

At first, she'd been thrilled to be free. But she hadn't settled and was so, so angry.

Annora figured she was entitled, after everything she'd been through. It would take time. Annora just wished the woman didn't have to keep suffering.

Then Thadd stepped out of the bathroom, and every thought flew out of her head.

When he'd told her that he'd be wearing traditional Zhalton battle dress to the ceremony, she hadn't given it much thought.

Now this, she could totally get behind.

His chest was bare. He wore a black battle skirt, with a heavy belt around his lean waist. A cool, curved knife hung from it. His broad, delicious chest only had a leather harness that crossed it diagonally. Intricate guards of beaten metal sat on his shoulders, and his vambraces were heavy, etched leather.

Rhain had given him a new sword. She knew that he was still sad about the one the Sarkans had taken. The new one looked similar, maybe a little longer. It currently sat in its sheath on his back.

"I want to fuck you," she said.

"Annora." A dull flush filled his cheeks. "I can't say it's a surprise. It's written all over your face."

She licked her lips. His gaze dropped to her mouth, then he took in her dress. Heat flared in his blue eyes.

She held out her hand. "No. We're the guests of honor. We can't be late."

He grunted. When he took her hand, she felt the tingle of energy between them. The sensation grew stronger and she liked it.

His fingers wound around hers. "I have something for you."

"What is it?"

"Two things actually." He strode to the carved bedside table. When he turned back to her, he held a flower in his hand.

It was white, elegant, but the stem was filled with thorns. It smelled divine.

"A *thistla* flower, for my *thistla*."

She took it carefully, smiling as she sniffed its fragrance. "It's beautiful. Even the thorns." She set it down on the table.

The second gift sat in the center of his big palm. The small, oval stone glowed gold.

"Oh?" She looked up. "What is it?"

"An energy stone mined on Zhalto. It's a tradition to give one to your love, to match the color of your energy."

Everything in her melted. "Thank you." She took the stone and carefully pulled the delicate chain she wore around her neck out from under her leather bodice. She clipped the stone on beside the charm from her sister.

He took her hand again. "Let's go, First Claw."

They left their quarters. Graylan's palace was built from a dark stone. It gleamed with veins of gold and silver running through it. The doorways and windows were all enormous, and the high-tech heating system kept the stone floors warm.

As they approached the throne room, Annora felt a twist of nerves.

Thadd sensed it, probably along their new bond. "You face down the Sarkans, the Zhylaw, prisoners on Krone—"

She shot him a look. "Annoying Zhaltons."

He smiled. He did it far more easily now. "But a little ceremony in your honor makes you nervous?"

"They're going to give us *medals*," she complained.

He squeezed her fingers. "Just enjoy your moment, Rahl. I'll be with you."

He would. Her chest loosened.

"Are you going to be this nervous when you meet my mother?" he asked.

Vague horror filled her. Annora had heard that the Countess Naveri was formidable. "Yes."

He laughed.

The large, burnished gold doors that lead into the

throne room were a work of art. They were flanked by two guards with expressionless faces, bodies clad in slick, black armor that gleamed under the light. They were two of Graylan's elite obsidian guards.

The man and woman opened the doors.

*By the claws.*

The huge room was filled with people. There were Talnians, Zhaltons, Damari. She spotted Tolf and some of the other cleavers among the crowd. The man winked at her.

As she and Thadd started down the aisle, the crowd erupted in applause and cheers.

*Oh.* She pressed her lips together. Thadd squeezed her fingers again.

They strode together. She spotted a smiling Carvia, and then a solemn Evie.

The woman from Earth looked lovely in a green dress. When she met Annora's gaze, she managed a small smile and held up a thumb. Annora assumed that was a good sign.

Then she turned to look at the top of the grand set of stairs.

Brodin and Rhain flanked Graylan. Brodin wore his intricate leather armor and Rhain was in battle dress like Thadd. Graylan was in all-black armor like his obsidian guards.

To the side stood Poppy and Mal. Poppy wore a swirl of green, the dress complementing her slender body. The color made Annora think of fresh leaves. Mal was in modified armor, with a fitted corset top and a straight skirt of deep blue.

The women both smiled at them.

Thadd and Annora stopped in front of the three warrior kings.

Graylan spoke. "Today, we're here to recognize extreme bravery, sacrifice, and courage. These two warriors stepped in to protect people who are not their own." He looked at Annora. "First Claw Rahl." He swiveled. "Captain Naveri. Damar, Zhalto, and Taln have a long history of being allies. You two went above and beyond for that alliance. You accepted a dangerous mission that almost cost you your lives. All to protect Taln and her people from evil." There was a faint ripple on Graylan's handsome face, and his gold eyes glowed. "An unforgiving evil. Words seem so inadequate," Graylan continued. "I don't have enough of them to express my thanks and gratitude. The thanks and gratitude of every Talnian."

"It's not necessary," Annora said. "We'd do it again. In a heartbeat. It's what's right."

"Not everyone does what's right. You're both honorable, noble, and brave." Graylan lifted a hand. A tall Talnian woman holding a tray walked over.

Graylan took the first medal and slipped it over Annora's head. It settled against her chest. He placed the second medal on Thadd.

She caught the look on Brodin's face. Pride. Rhain was looking at Thadd the same way.

She and Thadd turned. The roomful of people exploded in cheers.

"Well done, *thistla*," Thadd said.

"Back at you."

253

ANNA HACKETT

"We have a celebration feast planned," Graylan added.

*Great.* Annora just wanted to go back to her room with her man, and that very nice bed.

There was a sudden commotion in the crowd. People jostled and a woman screamed.

Then a sleek, dark wolf-dog bounded up the steps.

"What the—?" Brodin mumbled.

Pup leaped the last step and collided with Thadd. She wriggled until he stroked her head.

"A menace," Annora growled. The animal had been in the care of palace workers.

Pup glared at her.

Thadd slid an arm around Annora. "You'll always be my first love, Annora mine."

She stood proudly at her mate's side. For however long they lived, this man would walk beside her, love her, support her, drive her crazy.

She couldn't wait.

---

ALL THE INVITED Talnians partied in the throne room. Graylan had provided spiced wine and a spread of local delicacies.

Thadd was thankful to escape the huge party. The kings were having a smaller, private celebration upstairs.

The doors to the large balcony were open. There was a cool wind, but braziers burned outside, flames flickering in the breeze. Night had fallen, and Gearma was beautiful at night too. The city glowed gold against the dark mountains. Like gold coins spilling down the side of the hills.

An arm slid around him. "It's a party, Naveri. Loosen up." Annora leaned into him and handed him a glass of spiced wine.

"I'm good. I was admiring the view." He kissed the top of her head. "But you're even better to look at." There was the added bonus that she smelled divine. He didn't know what scent she was wearing, or if it was lotion rubbed on her smooth skin, but it was tormenting him.

"I knew you had some charm buried under the rugged exterior." Her gaze dropped to his medal. Hers rested against the bodice of her dress.

"They are pretty," she said.

"We didn't do the mission for any sort of recognition, but we earned these." He pressed his lips to hers. "When can we sneak out of here?"

She made a hungry sound. "Probably not yet."

"This is not the outcome I'd guessed when you two left Damari," a deep voice said.

They both looked up. Brodin looked bemused, a smiling Poppy tucked under his arm.

"It was *exactly* what I was hoping for," Poppy said. "If you didn't kill each other first."

Rhain and Mal joined them.

"Boy, you two have set some tongues wagging." Mal winked.

The overlord shook his head. "I knew you'd both set aside your...personal troubles to get the job done, but I didn't expect..."

"You guys to jump each other, have hot, delicious sex, and fall in love," Mal finished.

Rhain shot his woman a look. "As always, my love, you have a way with words."

"We didn't expect this either." Annora cocked her head to look at Thadd. "In hindsight, we always generated strong emotions in each other, and respected each other's work."

He cupped her cheek. "And I was always well aware you're gorgeous. I just thought you'd slice me with your claws if I told you."

That got low laughter from the others.

Annora's fingers danced over Thadd's jaw. "My mate."

"Mate?" A grin broke out on Brodin's rugged face. "Really? I'm thrilled for you."

"Wait, you aren't stealing my best friend and Captain of the Guard." Rhain glared at his brother.

Brodin's brows drew together. "And you aren't stealing my First Claw."

Annora held up a hand. "We've thought about this."

She and Thadd had talked about it over the last two days, trying to find a way to do the jobs they loved and still be with each other.

"We both have strong teams," Thadd said. "And we want to strengthen the alliance between our planets."

"We'd like to split our time," Annora said. "Half the year on each planet, and when we're both on one planet, our teams will be in charge on the other. We'll appoint a second to keep things running smoothly. Besides, the travel time between the planets isn't very long."

Both kings cocked their heads. For a second, it was easy to tell they were brothers.

"That could work," Brodin said.

"It could have other benefits as well," Rhain mused.

Mal elbowed him. "Quit thinking about strategic advantages. Your best friend is in love with a kick ass woman."

Rhain met Thadd's gaze. "I'm happy for you. You're one of the best men I know, and you deserve a good woman. You deserve to be happy."

Thadd's chest tightened. "Thanks, Rhain."

Brodin nodded. "I'm very happy for you."

Then Rhain's brow creased. "I am worried you'll miss the strong energy field of Zhalto. If you're away too long..."

Thadd cleared his throat. "I spoke with the medica today. Since...Krastin experimented on me, I've had fluctuations and changes in my powers."

Rhain's face darkened. "You should've said something."

"I was worried. I was keeping everything to myself." He glanced at the woman beside him. "Until someone forced me to accept it."

"You're okay?" Rhain asked. "I knew you were still suffering, but I didn't know how to help you."

Annora squeezed Thadd's arm, and Thadd looked at his overlord, his best friend. Rhain was a good friend.

"I've come to accept it." He looked at Annora. "And that those changes aren't bad. I can access my energy, strongly, wherever I am."

Rhain's brow shot up. "Really?"

Thadd nodded. "Really. I can tap into any energy supply."

"That's amazing. But I want one of the medicas to run more tests. Make sure it's safe."

"I'll talk to Tavith back on Zhalto." He was the head medica at Citadel.

"Good," Rhain said.

"Is everyone enjoying themselves?" Graylan arrived.

"The ceremony was unnecessary," Annora said.

"She hasn't forgiven you," Thadd said.

A smile touched Graylan's lips. "I know. True heroes don't like the recognition. But everyone on Taln appreciates what you both did, at great risk to yourselves. I appreciate it, and I can never thank you enough."

Thadd inclined his head. "Zavir won't stop."

Gray released a breath. "We know." He looked at his brothers, and they all shared a glance. When the conqueror looked back, gold gleamed in his eyes, like they were shot through with molten lava. "I will *never* stop protecting my planet."

There was a deadly edge to those words.

"As a clever woman has taught me, we're stronger together," Thadd said.

"We are." Gray's gaze moved over Thadd's shoulder. "And you made an unexpected discovery."

Thadd turned and followed Graylan's gaze across the room to Evie.

The Earth woman was sipping a drink, an unreadable look on her face. She didn't look like she was enjoying herself.

"She's been changed too," Thadd said. "She has abilities she didn't have before."

"And she's hurting," Annora added.

"She's coming back to Zhalto with us," Mal said. "She needs space and time to heal. She was a prisoner for two years. I don't know how she stayed sane."

"We'll all help her," Graylan said.

"Now, I'd like to dance with my soon-to-be queen," Rhain said, holding a hand out to Mal.

Thadd saw that Mal was getting better at hiding her wince at the queen word.

As the others drifted away, he slid an arm around his woman.

"I love you," he murmured.

She turned into his chest. "I want to hear that every day for the rest of our lives."

"Deal." He kissed her.

"Just leave me alone!" The feminine shout made the people nearby stop talking.

They turned and saw Evie facing off with Graylan.

She waved her hands at the conqueror. Gray said something, too low to hear, then Evie turned and stalked off.

A look of frustration crossed the conqueror's face.

"Space and time," Annora said. "And patience. We'll make sure she gets it."

Something barreled through the crowd. People let out startled exclamations.

"Oh no," Annora muttered.

Pup appeared, her claws screeching on the tile floor.

With a woof, the canine bounded to Thadd and sat on his boots. He rubbed the top of her head.

"We left that creature locked up in a spare bedroom with food," Annora said.

"She's clever."

"I suppose it's coming with us when we leave Taln?"

Pup growled at Annora.

"I think with some space and time, you and Pup will fall in love with each other," he said.

She rolled her eyes, then laughed. "It's always an adventure with you."

"It is. I wouldn't change anything. I want you right here at my side." He kissed her again. "Ready for a life together, First Claw?"

She bit his lip, love in her eyes. "Ready, my Captain."

---

I hope you enjoyed Annora and Thadd's story!

**GALACTIC KINGS** continues with **CONQUEROR** starring Conqueror Graylan Taln Sarkany and survivor Evie Mason, coming in late 2022.

If you'd like to know more about the Fortuna Station survivors on the desert planet of Carthago, then check out my action-packed science-fiction romance series, *Galactic Gladiators*. **Read on for a preview of *Gladiator*, the first book in Galactic Gladiators, starring Harper and Raiden.**

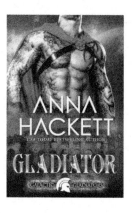

**Don't miss out!** For updates about new releases, action romance info, free books, and other fun stuff, sign up for my VIP mailing list and get your *free box set* containing three action-packed romances.

Visit here to get started: www.annahackett.com

## Would you like a FREE BOX SET of my books?

# PREVIEW: GLADIATOR

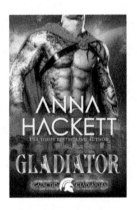

J ust another day at the office.

Harper Adams pulled herself along the outside of the space station module. She could hear her quiet breathing inside her spacesuit, and she easily pulled her weightless body along the slick, white surface of the module. She stopped to check a security panel, ensuring all the systems were running smoothly.

*Check.* Same as it had been yesterday, and the day

before that. But Harper never ever let herself forget that they were six hundred million kilometers away from Earth. That meant they were dependent only on themselves. She tapped some buttons on the security panel before closing the reinforced plastic cover. She liked to dot all her *I*s and cross all her *T*s. She never left anything to chance.

She grabbed the handholds and started pulling herself up over the cylindrical pod to check the panels on the other side. Glancing back behind herself, she caught a beautiful view of the planet below.

Harper stopped and made herself take it all in. The orange, white, and cream bands of Jupiter could take your breath away. Today, she could even see the famous superstorm of the Great Red Spot. She'd been on the Fortuna Research Station for almost eighteen months. That meant, despite the amazing view, she really didn't see it anymore.

She turned her head and looked down the length of the space station. At the end was the giant circular donut that housed the main living quarters and offices. The main ring rotated to provide artificial gravity for the residents. Lying off the center of the ring was the long cylinder of the research facility, and off that cylinder were several modules that housed various scientific labs and storage. At the far end of the station was the docking area for the supply ships that came from Earth every few months.

"Lieutenant Adams? Have you finished those checks?"

Harper heard the calm voice of her fellow space

marine and boss, Captain Samantha Santos, through the comm system in her helmet.

"Almost done," Harper answered.

"Take a good look at the botany module. The computer's showing some strange energy spikes, but the scientists in there said everything looks fine. Must be a system malfunction."

Which meant the geek squad engineers were going to have to come in and do some maintenance. "On it."

Harper swung her body around, and went feet-first down the other side of the module. She knew the rest of the security team—all made up of United Nations Space Marines—would be running similar checks on the other modules across the station. They had a great team to ensure the safety of the hundreds of scientists aboard the station. There was also a dedicated team of engineers that kept the guts of the station running.

She passed a large, solid window into the module, and could see various scientists floating around benches filled with all kinds of plants. They all wore matching gray jumpsuits accented with bright-blue at the collars, that indicated science team. There was a vast mix of scientists and disciplines aboard—biologists, botanists, chemists, astronomers, physicists, medical experts, and the list went on. All of them were conducting experiments, and some were searching for alien life beyond the edge of the solar system. It seemed like every other week, more probes were being sent out to hunt for radio signals or collect samples.

Since humans had perfected large solar sails as a way to safely and quickly propel spacecraft, getting around the solar system had become a lot easier. With radiation pressure exerted by sunlight onto the mirrored sails, they could travel from Earth to Fortuna Station orbiting Jupiter in just a few months. And many of the scientists aboard the station were looking beyond the solar system, planning manned expeditions farther and farther away. Harper wasn't sure they were quite ready for that.

She quickly checked the adjacent control panel. Among all the green lights, she spotted one that was blinking red, and she frowned. They definitely had a problem with the locking system on the exterior door at the end of the module. She activated the small propulsion pack on her spacesuit, and circled around the module. She slowed down as she passed the large, round exterior door at the end of the cylindrical module.

It was all locked into place and looked secure.

As she moved back to the module, she grabbed a handhold and then tapped the small tablet attached to the forearm of her suit. She keyed in a request for maintenance to come and check it.

She looked up and realized she was right near another window. Through the reinforced glass, a pretty, curvy blonde woman looked up and spotted Harper. She smiled and waved. Harper couldn't help but smile and lifted her gloved hand in greeting.

Dr. Regan Forrest was a botanist and a few years younger than Harper. The young woman was so open and friendly, and had befriended Harper from her first day on the station. Harper had never had a lot of friends —mainly because she'd been too busy raising her younger sister and working. She'd never had time for girly nights out or gossip.

But Regan was friendly, smart, and had the heart of a steamroller under her pretty exterior. Harper always had trouble saying no to her. Maybe the woman reminded her a little of Brianna. At the thought of her sister, something twisted painfully in Harper's chest.

Regan floated over to the window and held up a small tablet. She'd typed in some words.

*Cards tonight?*

Harper had been teaching Regan how to play poker. The woman was terrible at it, and Harper beat her all the time. But Regan never gave up.

Harper nodded and held up two fingers to indicate a couple of hours. She was off-shift shortly, and then she had a sparring match with Regan's cousin, Rory—one of the station engineers—in the gym. Aurora "Call me Rory or I'll hit you" Fraser had been trained in mixed martial arts, and Harper found the female engineer a hell of a sparring partner. Rory was teaching Harper some martial arts moves and Harper was showing the woman some basic sword moves. Since she was little, Harper had been a keen fencer.

Regan grinned back and nodded. Then the woman's wide smile disappeared. She spun around, and through the glass Harper could see the other scientists all looking around, concerned. One scientist was spinning around, green plants floating in the air around him, along with fat droplets of water and some other green fluid. He'd clearly screwed up and let his experiment get free.

"Lieutenant Adams?" The captain's voice came through her helmet again. "Harper?"

There was a sense of urgency that made Harper's belly tighten. "Go ahead, Captain."

"We have an alarm sounding in the botany module. The computer says there is a risk of decompression."

*Dammit.* "I just checked the security panels. The locking mechanism on the exterior door is showing red. I did a visual inspection and it's closed up tight."

"Okay, we talked with the scientist in charge. Looks like one of her team let something loose in there. It isn't dangerous, but it must be messing with the alarm sensors. System's locked them all in there." She made an annoyed sound. "Idiots will have to stay there until engineering can get down there and free them."

Harper studied the room through the glass again. Some of the green liquid had floated over to another bench that contained various frothing cylinders on it. A second later, the cylinders shattered, their contents bubbling upward.

The scientists all moved to the back exit of the module, banging on the locked door. *Damn.* They were trapped.

Harper met Regan's gaze. Her friend's face was pale, and wisps of her blonde hair had escaped her ponytail, floating around her face.

"Captain," Harper said. "Something's wrong. The experiments have overflowed their containment." She could see the scientists were all coughing.

"Engineering is on the way," the captain said.

Harper pushed herself off, flying over the surface of

the module. She reached the control panel and saw that several other lights had turned red. They needed to get this under control and they needed to do it now.

"Harper!" The captain's panicked voice. "Decompression in progress!"

*What the hell?* The module jerked beneath Harper. She looked up and saw the exterior door blow off, flying away from the station.

Her heart stopped. That meant all the scientists were exposed to the vacuum of space.

*Fuck.* Harper pushed off again, sending herself flying toward the end of the module. She put her arms by her sides to help increase her speed. Through the window, she saw that most of the scientists had grabbed on to whatever they could hold on to. A few were pulling emergency breathers over their heads.

She reached the end of the pod and saw the damage. There was torn metal where the door had been ripped off. Inside the door, she knew there would be a temporary repair kit containing a sheet of high-tech nano fabric that could be stretched across the opening to reestablish pressure. But it needed to be put in place manually. Harper reached for the latch to release the repair kit.

Suddenly, a slim body shot out of the pod, her arms and legs kicking. Her mouth was wide open in a silent scream.

*Regan.* Harper didn't let herself think. She turned, pushed off and fired her propulsion system, arrowing after her friend.

"Security Team to the botany module," she yelled through her comm system. "Security Team to botany module. We have decompression. One scientist has been expelled. I'm going after her. I need someone that can help calm the others and get the module sealed again."

"Acknowledged, Lieutenant," Captain Santos answered. "I'm on my way."

Harper focused on reaching Regan. She was gaining on her. She saw that the woman had lost consciousness. She also knew that Regan had only a couple of minutes to survive out here. Harper let her training take over. She tapped the propulsion system controls, trying for more speed, as she maneuvered her way toward Regan.

As she got close, Harper reached out and wrapped her arm around the scientist. "I've got you."

Harper turned, at the same time clipping a safety line to the loops on Regan's jumpsuit. Then, she touched the controls and propelled them straight back towards the module. She kept her friend pulled tightly toward her chest. *Hold on, Regan.*

She was so still. It reminded Harper of holding Brianna's dead body in her arms. Harper's jaw tightened. She wouldn't let Regan die out here. The woman had dreamed of working in space, and worked her entire career to get here, even defying her family. Harper wasn't going to fail her.

As the module got closer, she saw that the security team had arrived. She saw the captain's long, muscled body as she and another man put up the nano fabric.

"Incoming. Keep the door open."

"Can't keep it open much longer, Adams," the captain replied. "Make it snappy."

Harper adjusted her course, and, a second later, she

shot through the door with Regan in her arms. Behind her, the captain and another huge security marine, Lieutenant Blaine Strong, pulled the stretchy fabric across the opening.

"Decompression contained," the computer intoned.

Harper released a breath. On the panel beside the door, she saw the lights turning green. The nano fabric wouldn't hold forever, but it would do until they got everyone out of here, and then got a maintenance team in here to fix the door.

"Oxygen levels at required levels," the computer said again.

"Good work, Lieutenant." Captain Sam Santos floated over. She was a tall woman with a strong face and brown hair she kept pulled back in a tight ponytail. She had curves she kept ruthlessly toned, and golden skin she always said was thanks to her Puerto Rican heritage.

"Thanks, Captain." Harper ripped her helmet off and looked down at Regan.

Her blonde hair was a wild tangle, her face was pale and marked by what everyone who worked in space called space hickeys—bruises caused by the skin's small blood vessels bursting when exposed to the vacuum of space. *Please be okay.*

"Here." Blaine appeared, holding a portable breather. The big man was an excellent marine. He was about six foot five with broad shoulders that stretched his spacesuit to the limit. She knew he was a few inches over the height limit for space operations, but he was a damn good marine, which must have gone in his favor. He had dark skin thanks to his African-American father and his handsome face made him popular with the station's single ladies, but mostly he worked and hung out with the other marines.

"Thanks." Harper slipped the clear mask over Regan's mouth.

"Nice work out there." Blaine patted her shoulder. "She's alive because of you."

Suddenly, Regan jerked, pulling in a hard breath.

"You're okay." Harper gripped Regan's shoulder. "Take it easy."

Regan looked around the module, dazed and panicky. Harper watched as Regan caught sight of the fabric stretched across the end of the module, and all the plants floating around inside.

"God," Regan said with a raspy gasp, her breath fogging up the dome of the breather. She shook her head, her gaze moving to Harper. "Thanks, Harper."

"Any time." Harper squeezed her friend's shoulder. "It's what I'm here for."

Regan managed a wan smile. "No, it's just you. You didn't have to fly out into space to rescue me. I'm grateful."

"Come on. We need to get you to the infirmary so they can check you out. Maybe put some cream on your hickeys."

"Hickeys?" Regan touched her face and groaned. "Oh, no. I'm going to get a ribbing."

"And you didn't even get them the pleasurable way."

A faint blush touched Regan's cheeks. "That's right. If I had, at least the ribbing would have been worth it."

With a relieved laugh, Harper looked over at her captain. "I'm going to get Regan to the infirmary."

The other woman nodded. "Good. We'll meet you back at the Security Center."

With a nod, Harper pushed off, keeping one arm around Regan, and they floated into the main part of the science facility. Soon, they moved through the entrance into the central hub of the space station. As the artificial gravity hit, Harper's boots thudded onto the floor. Beside her, Regan almost collapsed.

Harper took most of the woman's weight and helped her down the corridor. They pushed into the infirmary.

A gray-haired, barrel-chested man rushed over. "Decided to take an unscheduled spacewalk, Dr. Forrest?"

Regan smiled weakly. "Yes. Without a spacesuit."

The doctor made a tsking sound and then took her from Harper. "We'll get her all patched up."

Harper nodded. "I'll come and check on you later."

Regan grabbed her hand. "We have a blackjack game scheduled. I'm planning to win back all those chocolates you won off me."

Harper snorted. "You can try." It was good to see some life back in Regan's blue eyes.

As Harper strode out into the corridor, she ran a hand through her dark hair, tension slowly melting out of her shoulders. She really needed a beer. She tilted her neck one way and then the other, hearing the bones pop.

*Just another day at the office.* The image of Regan drifting away from the space station burst in her head.

Harper released a breath. She was okay. Regan was safe and alive. That was all that mattered.

With a shake of her head, Harper headed toward the Security Center. She needed to debrief with the captain and clock off. Then she could get out of her spacesuit and take the one-minute shower that they were all allotted.

That was the one thing she missed about Earth. Long, hot showers.

And swimming. She'd been a swimmer all her life and there were days she missed slicing through the water.

She walked along a long corridor, meeting a few people—mainly scientists. She reached a spot where there was a long bank of windows that afforded a lovely view of Jupiter, and space beyond it.

Stingy showers and unscheduled spacewalks aside, Harper had zero regrets about coming out into space. There'd been nothing left for her on Earth, and to her surprise, she'd made friends here on Fortuna.

As she stared out into the black, mesmerized by the twinkle of stars, she caught a small flash of light in the distance. She paused, frowning. What the hell was that?

She stared hard at the spot where she'd seen the flash. Nothing there but the pretty sprinkle of stars. Harper shook her head. Fatigue was playing tricks on her. It had to have just been a weird trick of the lights reflecting off the glass.

Pushing the strange sighting away, she continued on to the Security Center.

## Galactic Gladiators
Gladiator

273

ANNA HACKETT

Warrior

Hero

Protector

Champion

Barbarian

Beast

Rogue

Guardian

Cyborg

Imperator

Hunter

Also Available as Audiobooks!

# PREVIEW: EON WARRIORS AND HELL SQUAD

L ooking for more action-packed science fiction romance? Check out *Eon Warriors,* starting with the first book in the series is *Edge of Eon.*

**Framed for a crime she didn't commit, a wrongly-imprisoned space captain's only chance at freedom is to abduct a fearsome alien war commander.**

Sub-Captain Eve Traynor knows a suicide mission when she sees one. With deadly insectoid aliens threatening to invade Earth, the planet's only chance of survival is to get the attention of the fierce Eon Warriors. But the Eon want nothing to do with Earth, and Eve wants nothing to do with abducting War Commander Davion Thann-Eon off his warship. But when Earth's Space Corps threaten her sisters, Eve will do anything to keep them safe, even if it means she might not make it back.

War Commander Davion Thann-Eon is taking his first vacation in years. Dedicated to keeping the Eon Empire safe, he's been born and bred to protect. But when he's attacked and snatched off his very own warship, he is shocked to find himself face-to-face with a bold, tough little Terran warrior. One who both infuriates and intrigues him.

When their shuttle is attacked by the ravenous insectoid Kantos, Eve and Davion crash land on the terrifying hunter planet known as Hunter7. A planet designed to test a warrior to his limits. Now, the pair must work together to survive, caught between the planet and its dangers, the Kantos hunting them down, and their own incendiary attraction.

### Eon Warriors
Edge of Eon
Touch of Eon
Heart of Eon
Kiss of Eon
Mark of Eon
Claim of Eon
Storm of Eon

Soul of Eon
King of Eon
Also Available as Audiobooks!

Want to learn more about *Hell Squad*? Check out the first action-packed book in the series, *Marcus*.

**In the aftermath of a deadly alien invasion, a band of survivors fights on…**

In a world gone to hell, Elle Milton—once the darling of the Sydney social scene—has carved a role for herself as the communications officer for the toughest commando team fighting for humanity's survival—Hell Squad. It's her chance to make a difference and make up for horrible past mistakes…despite the fact that its battle-hardened commander never wanted her on his team.

When Hell Squad is tasked with destroying a strategic alien facility, Elle knows they need her skills in the field. But first she must go head to head with Marcus Steele and convince him she won't be a liability.

Marcus Steele is a warrior through and through. He fights to protect the innocent and give the human race a chance to survive. And that includes the beautiful, gutsy Elle who twists him up inside with a single look. The last thing he wants is to take her into a warzone, but soon they are thrown together battling both the alien invaders and their overwhelming attraction. And Marcus will learn just how much he'll sacrifice to keep her safe.

## Hell Squad

Marcus

Cruz

Gabe

Reed

Roth

Noah

Shaw

Holmes

Niko

Finn

Devlin

Theron

Hemi

Ash

Levi

Manu

Griff

Dom

Survivors

Tane

Also Available as Audiobooks!

# ALSO BY ANNA HACKETT

Mission: Her Shield

Mission: Her Justice

Also Available as Audiobooks!

## **Treasure Hunter Security**

Undiscovered

Uncharted

Unexplored

Unfathomed

Untraveled

Unmapped

Unidentified

Undetected

Also Available as Audiobooks!

## **Galactic Kings**

Overlord

Emperor

Captain of the Guard

## **Eon Warriors**

Edge of Eon

Touch of Eon

Heart of Eon

Kiss of Eon

Mark of Eon

Claim of Eon

Storm of Eon

Soul of Eon

King of Eon

Also Available as Audiobooks!

## Galactic Gladiators: House of Rone

Sentinel

Defender

Centurion

Paladin

Guard

Weapons Master

Also Available as Audiobooks!

## Galactic Gladiators

Gladiator

Warrior

Hero

Protector

Champion

Barbarian

Beast

Rogue

Guardian

Cyborg

Imperator

Hunter

Also Available as Audiobooks!

## Hell Squad

Marcus

Cruz

Gabe

Reed

Roth

Noah

Shaw

Holmes

Niko

Finn

Devlin

Theron

Hemi

Ash

Levi

Manu

Griff

Dom

Survivors

Tane

Also Available as Audiobooks!

## The Anomaly Series

Time Thief

Mind Raider

Soul Stealer

Salvation

Anomaly Series Box Set

## The Phoenix Adventures

Among Galactic Ruins

At Star's End

In the Devil's Nebula

On a Rogue Planet

Beneath a Trojan Moon

Beyond Galaxy's Edge

On a Cyborg Planet

Return to Dark Earth

On a Barbarian World

Lost in Barbarian Space

Through Uncharted Space

Crashed on an Ice World

## Perma Series

Winter Fusion

A Galactic Holiday

**Warriors of the Wind**

Tempest

Storm & Seduction

Fury & Darkness

**Standalone Titles**

Savage Dragon

Hunter's Surrender

One Night with the Wolf

For more information visit www.annahackett.com

## ABOUT THE AUTHOR

I'm a USA Today bestselling romance author who's passionate about *fast-paced, emotion-filled* contemporary romantic suspense and science fiction romance. I love writing about people overcoming unbeatable odds and achieving seemingly impossible goals. I like to believe it's possible for all of us to do the same.

I live in Australia with my own personal hero and two very busy, always-on-the-move sons.

For release dates, behind-the-scenes info, free books, and other fun stuff, sign up for the latest news here:

Website: www.annahackett.com